THE SPIDER:
KING OF THE FLESHLESS LEGION

MASTER OF MEN!

THE SPIDER®

KING OF THE
FLESHLESS LEGION

By Grant Stockbridge

POPULAR PUBLICATIONS • 2022

CHAPTER 1
DEATH AT MIDNIGHT

THE ANGRY roar of the mob was ominous in the softness of the spring night. Its first sullen rumble changed as it swept closer to high-tossing waves of furious sound. Hurrying rapidly along Sutton Place, Richard Wentworth checked to peer narrowly through the midnight dark toward Second Avenue where the violence seemed to center.

"Hurry on, Nita," he urged the woman who clung to his arm. "Get to the drugstore phone. Tell the police to make all possible speed. It's serious."

Nita van Sloan hesitated at Wentworth's side, her white hand sensing the tautening of the lithe muscles of his arm while her eyes took in the increasing gravity of his hawkish profile. She shivered a little at the bestial quality of the mob howl.

"Dick, promise you won't do anything… foolish. Remember, you're unarmed."

"Yes, yes—hurry, dear." Wentworth waved her on without turning his eyes from the corner where he thought the mob would show first.

In heaven's name, what could send men marching so fiercely through the soft night of spring? He must find their object, turn them aside until the police came or someone might be hurt. It was typical of the man, that echo of his thoughts. *Someone might be hurt.* He did not think of danger to himself, only of the possible service he might render.

Nita was running now, her sables flung wide, her silver gown caught high about her silken knees. The gem-glittering heels of her slippers clicked out sharp explosions of sound against the pavement. There was need to hurry. A long cross-town block away, the mob was turning the corner toward where Wentworth stood!

Wentworth swore softly as he watched the thick-pressed ranks of the men swell like a monstrous black serpent around the distant corner. Even from this distance, he could feel the impact of their single-minded hatred. It was like a tangible thing. It beat in upon him with the fresher, wilder surge of their voices. Then a single, thinner sound cut across it... a woman's scream. *Nita's scream!*

Wentworth's head whipped about and he saw Nita, poised in rigid fright before the pharmacy. Her white arms were twisted defensively before her face as if she would thrust her backward-arching body away from some horror behind the doors. The neon sign smeared bloody light across the swirling silver of her dress.

An instant, Wentworth hesitated, then glass crashed from the pharmacy entrance, one door swung outward a little way, flung back. With a suppressed shout, Wentworth hurled himself into a sprint.

"Coming, Nita," he shouted.

As if she gained courage from his voice, Nita took a slow step

toward the door. She had time for no more before Wentworth reached her and peered in through the shattered glass.

Just inside, a man crouched in a tortured posture of agonized pain. His hat lay on the floor, and there was blood upon his scalp where his head had smashed against the glass. Slowly, as Wentworth stared, the man's head twisted upward. His face was hideously distorted. His eyes puckered and his lips shrank back from his teeth. Even as Wentworth sprang forward, the man slipped to the floor. His limbs writhed in slow contortions and a tearing groan squeezed out between his locked teeth.

"Quickly," Wentworth shouted at the druggist. "A hypodermic needle. Strychnine. Hurry, man. He's dying!"

The druggist was leaning across the counter, both hands planted there, his whole body shaking. His thin, pale face was sagging in astonishment… Nita sprang toward him, repeating Wentworth's order, and the man staggered away from the counter, began to fumble in drawers. Nita snatched the things from under his awkward hands.

"What's the matter?" the druggist was panting. "Oh, what's the matter? He just asked for a drink and now…."

Nita had the hypodermic filled and she ran back to Wentworth's side. The man's face was mottled, purplish with congested blood. Wentworth ripped open his vest and shirt, plunged the needle home with deft hands. For an instant, the man's eyes flared wide. He stared up into Wentworth's kindly, intent face.

"Poison!" the man gasped. "I've been…" He shuddered and a terrific convulsion made his body writhe.

Nita's hand gripped Wentworth's shoulder achingly. "Oh," she whispered. "Oh, he's… dying."

Wentworth shook his head and pushed heavily to his feet. "He's dead," he said, and his head lifted sharply. The mob-howl… Lord, it was just outside! Men's feet were tramping heavily and he could make out individual sharp shouts.

"Lynch him!" a hoarse voice bellowed. *"Lynch the poisoner!"*

The druggist had come stumblingly forward and stood wringing small, ineffective hands. "Oh, what's the matter?" he whispered. "I haven't done anything. I haven't, so help me God. The man just came in and asked for something for a headache. I gave him one of those fizz drinks, and… He was just a customer. I…."

Wentworth's keen eyes probed the pharmacist's weak face. "Know this man?" he demanded.

The druggist backed away, flapping his hands. "I never saw him before. He just came in and asked for a drink, and…."

"Hide," Wentworth ordered sharply. "Nita, phone the police. Try to find a back way out of this place. I'll hold off this mob. It looks very much as if someone else had been poisoned by drugs from this place today." Nita was already hurrying toward the phone booth. "Don't let him get away," Wentworth ordered grimly. "He'll have some questions to answer. If you can reach the house…."

A side window crashed and a half-brick bounded across the store, smashed heavily through a showcase. The druggist squealed and ran. Wentworth reached the door in two long strides and stepped outside to face the mob as it trooped toward him. His hands were empty; he was unarmed… He lifted both arms there, a tall, commanding figure with an intense, intelligent face. He was in evening dress and when he lifted his arms the light topcoat he wore swung open.

"Just a moment, men," he said quietly. "What's the matter here?"

HIS CALM eyes swept over the mob. There were fully a score of men with clubs in their hands; their faces were ugly with rage. He tried to pick out their leader and his gaze centered on a broad-shouldered workingman in the front ranks.

"You tell me," Wentworth ordered. "What's the matter? Don't you realize you're apt to get in trouble like this?"

"Trouble?" The man's voice was heavy and thick. "Trouble? What the hell do I care? That man... that man in there..." He shook his great, empty fists. "He kill my two babies! He kill my wife!" He surged forward and behind him the mob moved with the singleness of a great, many-legged beast... Wentworth went to meet the man, smiling, arms hanging idly at his sides.

"Wait a minute," he urged. "Tell me about it. How did this happen?"

He was playing desperately for time. If he could get this man to expend his rage in words... There was horror here. This was more than a deadly mistake on the pharmacist's part in making up a prescription. There was this other man, dead on the floor, to testify to that! In God's name, what was happening here? From somewhere in the mob, a brick was hurled. The breath of its passage fanned Wentworth's cheek and behind him glass crashed again! Wentworth's smile did not waver; nor did he dodge from the missile.

"Tell me about it," he repeated to the bereaved man. "I'll see that justice is done."

"Don't listen to him!" a voice bawled out. "He's in with the crooks! Knock him down!"

This time, Wentworth spotted the man who spoke and a cold fire began to burn in his eyes. Years of underworld warfare had taught him that there was no such thing as a criminal type. Yet they had one thing in common, these men who extorted an underhanded living from the innocent—a brazen egotism and a callousness toward human suffering that must always leave its mark. That brand was upon the sly, furtive face of the man who shouted... and then promptly hid behind someone else when Wentworth's eyes sought him out.

"You, there!" Wentworth singled him out. "What have you got to do with this? Trying to make trouble for other people?"

"You're all alike." The man shouted, still hiding behind one of the mob. "You rich guys gang together! Trying to stomp us under your iron heel! Bloody capitalists!"

"Come and tell me about it," Wentworth urged, his voice soft. "You other men. You don't want to get in trouble with the law! If this druggist has caused deaths, he'll pay the penalty. You know you can count on that!"

As he spoke, he deserted his post in front of the door and was shouldering his way straight in among the angry men. Clubs were lifted threateningly... Wentworth did not even look at those who menaced him. His eyes were boring into the furtive eyes of this criminal who, he knew now, was the leader. Why didn't the police come? Surely, there had been time for at least one radio car to reach the spot… unless the phone wires had been cut!

That was pure conjecture, of course, but there was something damnably suspicious about this combination of circumstances. Four deaths from this one drugstore; a mob deliberately organized by this criminal—and the police late in coming! Abruptly, Wentworth knew that his premonitions were correct. The underworld had been quiet too long and now it was stirring at last! What horror those roiling depths soon would bring to the surface he could not guess. But he did feel convinced that he was dealing with one of its first manifestations.

"Listen, men," Wentworth moved forward, thoughts racing through his keen brain. "If you harm this druggist—no matter with what justification—the law will get you. You'll pay the penalty. This man who is urging you on, will run away and get off free. Why don't you ask him what he has to do with all this? Ask him *why* he cares…."

If only he could turn the attention of the mob to this one man, away from the drugstore… He could count on Nita getting to a phone soon even if those in the pharmacy wires had been cut. But she would need time.

"*You're* the real criminal." Wentworth was within a dozen feet of the man he had singled out *"Tell them who paid you to do this!"* WENTWORTH SAW amazement and fear change the man's small-mouthed furtive face and it was all the confirmation he needed. He had guessed right!

"He's trying to trick you!" the man shouted. "Look, he's the owner of that store! I know him! He's just trying to trick you!

Knock him down…" The man's hand flitted across his chest and stabbed under his coat lapel in a gesture Wentworth knew all too well. He would shoot without hesitation—and Wentworth was unarmed!

It was because Wentworth had approached so quietly, so fearlessly, that he had been able to enter the thick press of the mob without injury. Now, he was more afraid for these men about him than for himself. An almost superstitious fear was shaking the gunman, and when his weapon was free, he would shoot… without discrimination, blindly. The instant the man's hand moved in that betraying gesture, Wentworth was in action. A quick reach of his hand caught a club from the fist of the nearest mobster and a continuation of the same movement hurled it straight at the face of the gunman!

The man, pulling his gun, almost succeeded in dodging the hurriedly thrown club. As he ducked aside, it grazed past his cheek, tore his ear. With a yelp, he flung up his left arm defensively and tried to jerk his gun into line.

Wentworth's leaping dive, started just as he flung the club, carried him headlong into the man's body. His smashing shoulder drove out the man's wind and, in the next instant, Wentworth was on his feet, the captured gun in hand. He hit once, knocking out the criminal, but he did not level the gun at the mob.

"All right, men," Wentworth said quietly. "I've got the troublemaker. The rest of you can go home and the police will see that the men responsible for these deaths are punished. I promise you that!"

The clubs were sagging in the men's hands now. That swift, efficient action, the gun in Wentworth's hand, had a calming effect. Near the doors of the store, Wentworth could see the bereaved father whose poisoned family had been the excuse for this outbreak. His heavy shoulders were bowed, his head sagging....

Wentworth felt anger surging through his own veins. Damn the criminals who could cause such tragedies out of greed! What their exact purpose was, Wentworth could not guess, but he would find out! The Spider must take again the trail of justice!

"Yeah, you're promising us," a man's hoarse voice broke in on Wentworth's thoughts. "*You're* promising us! Who are you?"

Wentworth smiled slightly. "You may know my name," he said. "Richard Wentworth."

His challenger's eyes widened. "Geez, yes, I know you. Sure, and—"

A shot slashed across the muted mutter of the crowd. It came from some distance away and at its sharp report—Richard Wentworth pitched forward to the pavement.

CHAPTER 2
SKELETON WITHOUT ARMS

S HOUTS OF fright burst from the crowd at Wentworth's fall. For a moment, the men stood motionless, peering toward the car from which the shot had come. Then a hail of bullets whined toward them. One man screamed and, bent double, pitched writhing to the pavement. Another dropped without a sound. It was enough. With screams, the others broke into furious flight, scattering toward the dark safety of doorways and side streets.

On the ground lay four men, the two members of the mob felled by bullets; the unconscious leader… and Richard Wentworth. The death car rolled toward them slowly and the metal of guns glinted at the windows; the white blurs of alert faces peered out. Wentworth had not seemed to move since his fall, but his hand remained tightly on the butt of his captured automatic. His head was turned so that he faced the approaching car. From its windows, the guns began to spit again. Two weapons were firing deliberately. The body of the man beside Wentworth jerked to the prodding leaden bullets.

Abruptly, another gun sent its crashing echoes along the street. From a dark doorway, splinters of powder flame stabbed out into the night, reaching toward the sedan. A policeman, perhaps? But there had been no skirling of an alarm whistle… Wentworth smiled thinly as he deliberately lifted his automatic into line on the sedan. Whoever the unknown gun-fighter was, Wentworth now owed him a great debt.

Wentworth was as deliberate as if he stood on a target range. He dropped his muzzle into line on the windshield where he could see the white blur of the driver's face… Then a startled cry leaped to his lips! A man in the rear was crouching near the window, his right arm drawn back to throw… something. Went-

The flaming sedan leaped the curb
and smashed down an iron fence!

worth could barely glimpse the enlarged silhouette of his fist, but he did not need to see the object the man held. It was a bomb!

If the man succeeded in throwing that bomb, it meant death to himself and the criminal he had taken prisoner... It meant worse than that—death to Nita where she guarded the druggist in his store! Wentworth's heart was pounding in his throat but his gun-hand did not tremble. A twist of the wrist and the gun was bearing on that rear window. No time for nice aiming now, nor for picking a careful target. The man was in the window, and the bomb in his fist was in range. With a trigger finger timed to the exact top speed of fire for the automatic, Wentworth raked that window from side to side with lead. The gun jumped in his hand like a miniature machine-gun, and....

Red and white flame streaked outward through the car windows! It thrust jagged fingers up through holes torn instantly in the roof! Behind Wentworth, the windows of the drugstore collapsed in final ruin as concussion swept over him in a great wind. It sucked the breath from his lungs and left him half-stunned. Only the urgency of his will drove him, reeling, to his feet, sent him staggering toward the drugstore even while his blurred eyes held the car. The gun in his hand was empty....

At the blast, the sedan leaped like a heart-shot deer, slammed down to veer drunkenly across the street. It leaped the curb, smashed down an iron guard-fence and dropped its front wheels into a basement-entrance well. Wentworth heard the crash dully in blast-muted ears, and thereafter not any sound at all. Not even a scream....

WENTWORTH WAS already pushing toward the drugstore, his pace a shambling run as he forced his stunned senses to coordination. His one thought was to locate Nita. He couldn't be sure whether the shrilling in his ears was from the explosion or whether police at last were closing in... Ardently as he had longed for the police earlier in the affair, he did not want them now.

If he could get the druggist and the unconscious gunman, he had left in the street, back to his own house, he thought he could swiftly get to the bottom of the night's horror. Criminals knew that the police were hampered in their attempts to force out the truth; about a man like Wentworth they could not know.

There had been, time and again, rumors and stories in the newspapers which linked Wentworth's name with that of the dread lone wolf of justice whom all the underworld feared with an awful fear, the Spider. No one, save his few closest intimates, knew Wentworth's perilous secret—that he was indeed that swift nemesis of criminals whose guns had brought low so many enemies of society. But his captive would wonder... And Wentworth's Sikh body servant. Ram Singh, had a terrifyingly persuasive way of handling his long-bladed knives....

These thoughts were muddling through Wentworth's mind even as he plunged through the drugstore entrance, a mess of splintered glass now. Nita should be all right unless one of those bullets had gone astray, and....

"Nita!" Wentworth called sharply. "Nita, are you all right?"

He stopped at the counter, listening. There were bullet holes in the glass that shielded the telephone booth and, on a shelf, a broken bottle dribbled the last of its contents on the floor. There was a pungent odor of spilled chemicals.

"*Nita!*" Wentworth cried. He flung himself around the counter and into the prescription room. The phone booth… He dared a glance… Empty, thank God! The prescription room was empty also. Then Wentworth saw a high square window that swung open, and under it a chair had been placed on the counter. Thankfulness flooded through Wentworth's heart. It had been as he had hoped. Nita must have failed to reach the police and had left that way to get help. She would have the druggist with her.

There was no mistake now about the sirens. They were still faint with distance, but they could close the interval quickly, as Wentworth well knew. He looped about, moving more surely now and plunged toward the front of the drugstore. He caught up a bottle from the soda fountain and a glass. He wanted to check on what had poisoned that customer and… good Lord! Out there in the street, a man was stooping over the unconscious criminal.

"Stay just like that!" Wentworth ordered sharply and leveled his empty automatic. "Let that gun fall!"

The man twisted a white, youthful face about, managed a smile. "It's all right," he said. "I'm not one of the gunmen."

Wentworth closed up the distance with long strides and his gray-blue eyes took the summary of the man in a single keen glance. Brown eyes looked back at him steadily, and the lips, smiling above a clean-cut chin, were wide and generous… Wentworth remembered that someone else had been returning

16

the fire of the killers. It might very well have been this man, but he could take no chances with an empty gun in his hand.

"Drop the gun," he repeated quietly. "We can discuss the rest afterward."

The man's smile tightened, but he obeyed. "Aren't you Richard Wentworth?" he asked hurriedly. "I've seen pictures of you. Look, I'm Donald Beck, a private detective. I was coming to see you tomorrow with a proposition and I came up here tonight to... to make sure of where you lived."

The man stammered a little over his explanation and Wentworth continued to regard him with searching steadiness. Donald Beck, private detective... perhaps. It was also possible that he had been planted here to make sure of Wentworth if the others failed. Slowly a smile curved Wentworth's grim-set lips. He would soon find out, and if this man were involved with the criminals... why there was one more source of information!

"Very well," Wentworth said quietly, "you can make me the proposition at my home. Meantime, just get that man's body on your shoulders and walk ahead of me, Mr. Donald Beck. If I find you're telling the truth, I won't be ungrateful. If you aren't...."

For seconds, Beck continued to meet Wentworth's probing eyes. There was a slight flush in his cheeks, but his voice was steady enough. "Very well, sir," he said. With smooth power, he seized the gunman's inert body, pulled it to a sitting position and, stooping, heaved it across his shoulders. "Which way?"

Wentworth felt a broadening smile tug at his lips. Beck had courage, at any rate. He directed him into the side street, on which the steel-guarded gates of his fortress-home opened,

17

and followed at a jog trot after scooping up Beck's gun. The sirens were very near; there was no time to be lost... and in the back of Wentworth's mind was a hot point of worry. If only he could be sure Nita was safe... Lord, what an end to an evening that had started out as a pleasant little social gathering to honor Nita's
visiting cousin from the South—Melissa Moulin was her name.

This furious violence had started as a quiet stroll along Sutton Place after all of the guests had left save young Forbes who was calling on Melissa... a stroll, just Dick and Nita together in the spring night. It had been a blissful relief from weeks and months of constant warfare. A relief? Wentworth laughed sharply.

He whipped a small silver whistle from his pocket and, eyes on his wrist-watch as he loped along, he blew a peculiar intermittent and perfectly timed cadence of notes. Just ahead of Beck, the close-fitting steel gates of Wentworth's fortress home, which he had built partly on filled land between two piers over the East River, slid silently apart—operated by sonic-actuated electric motors. Wentworth saw Beck hesitate and shouldered him through. Instantly, the gates were closing again and, as their muted thud ran through the dark courtyard before Wentworth's home, the sirens shrieked to a crescendo and died a half-block away. The police had arrived.

"You'll pardon my precipitancy," Wentworth told Beck dryly, "but I have some questions to ask before we give the police the details of the evening."

A brawny, turbaned Sikh was hurrying toward them from the shielded lights of the building's entrance.

Wentworth motioned to him. "Conduct this gentlemen, Mr. Beck, and his charge to the laboratory, Ram Singh," Wentworth directed. "Has Miss Nita come back or phoned?"

"No, *sahib,* " the Sikh replied gutturally. "Jackson went to seek thee when we heard the noises. He left just before the explosion. Hadst thou not ordered thy servant to remain on guard, I, too...."

"Jackson left?" Wentworth said slowly. "Curious that I didn't meet or see him, still..." His frown lifted. He was intensely worried over the failure to hear from Nita, but perhaps Jackson, his other close comrade in the Spider's work—his chauffeur to the world—had found Nita and was helping her.

"Full protection, Ram Singh," he ordered.

"Han, sahib." The Sikh salaamed in acknowledgment of the order that would set the hundred electric robots at work guarding the place against surprise or invasion. From now on, no one could approach within twenty-five feet of the walls without sounding an alarm, without automatically turning on blazing floodlights and setting up defensive electric circuits in steel gates and steel-crested walls. The voltage would not kill, but it would knock a man out.

For an instant, Wentworth stood there in the darkness of the wall-enclosed courtyard with its soft tinkling fountain and its carefully tended flowers and shrubs. The softness of spring still came to him and mellow whooping of tugs on the East River, just behind his home.

But there was no pleasure for Wentworth in the budding of the year; there could be only cold caution and ceaseless warfare, for he knew with an assurance built upon years of such battling that the night's outbreak was no isolated case. Another power was burgeoning in the underworld; another evil brain was plotting against the peace and safety and happiness of the people. For Wentworth, the tocsin had sounded and once more the Spider must tread in perilous ways where every man's hand was turned against him; where his only friend was the swift death that waited in his guns… God, if only he knew Nita was safe!

Wentworth swung toward the formal double doors which gave entrance to the ground floor of his home, and, just inside the elegant simplicity of the foyer, he stopped. A man was coming toward him from the elevators, and the man was frowning….

"Oh, Mr. Wentworth," he said. "I'm glad to see you again before I left. I was quite worried about you… all that shooting in the streets, but I hesitated to call the police."

"Quite all right, Mr. Forbes," Wentworth told him. "Good of you to stay and keep Miss Moulin company." He had forgotten the man was in the house, had stayed to keep Nita's cousin company while he and Nita went for their stroll.

His eyes swept the man's long, somewhat dour face, probed the gaze behind the rimless nose-glasses. How long had Forbes been in the foyer here and had he seen Wentworth's prisoner? If he had, it was best that he shouldn't be questioned by the police quite yet.

Wentworth said slowly, "You're quite a student of toxicological analysis, aren't you, Mr. Forbes?"

Forbes' full lips moved in a smile, "Oh, I dabble a little in poisons. There isn't much time for it at the Eastern Drug Company's laboratories. Did I tell you I'd shifted there recently?"

Wentworth controlled a start and slowly lifted the bottle he had in his hand. It contained Aspo-Seltzer, the drink which the drugstore customer had taken just before he died—and it was made in the Eastern Drug laboratories!

He said quietly, "I wonder if I could trouble you to run an analysis on this stuff here in my lab now? It just happens to be made by the company you work for. And a man who drank it died!"

Forbes uttered a startled exclamation. "Not the man you were just carrying in here?"

Wentworth shook his head quietly. "No, I think he may be involved in the death, that's all." He masked the quick suspicion in his eyes behind a smile. Forbes apparently had not intended to mention seeing his prisoner… until it was startled out of him.

"I gave Ram Singh a bit of a new restorative we're working on in the lab," Forbes was saying rapidly. "I wanted to stay and see how it worked, but Ram Singh is not… exactly affable. I didn't know… How sure are you it was this Aspo-Seltzer that poisoned the man? Lord, old man Wister will be frantic if this ever gets out!"

Wentworth noted mentally that Samuel Wister was head of the Eastern Drug Company and led Forbes to the laboratory to run the tests on the drug. Ram Singh was working over the prisoner on a cot where Wentworth sometimes napped during experiments of his own. It was a small room off the laboratory.

Beck was standing by, frowning. He looked up as Wentworth came in.

"I've seen this man somewhere before," he said, "but I can't place him. Probably on a 'wanted' list."

"Probably," Wentworth agreed. "Beck, it will be a little while before I have an opportunity to talk with you. Would you mind waiting in the next room?"

Beck moved toward the laboratory and, with a jerk of his head, Wentworth indicated to Ram Singh that he was to keep watch. Then he stood staring down at the criminal who had been inciting the mob.

IN RELAXATION, all the sly, evil lines of the man's face seemed to be emphasized. His mouth was loose, ugly. It twitched with the first hint of returning consciousness. Swiftly, Wentworth searched the man's pockets, found nothing of importance until he patted the coat and located a narrow, hidden recess close to the hem. From it, he drew an object that brought a keen look to his eyes.

A surprising thing for a criminal to carry in a secret pocket. It looked like a child's Halloween favor, a tiny skeleton carved out of wood with legs and arms made out of spring wire so that they bobbed and quivered in a pseudo life-like manner. The right arm was missing… Wentworth weighed it on his palm. No question that this was some sort of criminal talisman, or identification emblem.

It was significant that a skeleton was used—and that the victims of these criminals had died of drugs from bottles which should have borne the skull-and-cross-bones symbol of poison and, tragically, did *not!* Wentworth's hand closed into a knotted fist about the tiny skeleton. His prisoner was opening his eyes....

In a stride, Wentworth caught up a bottle on which glared the red skull-and-crossbones label of poison. He held it idly in his hand where the man's eyes would find it when they came to focus... Abruptly, the man swore and his hand ducked toward the empty holster beneath his arm. He cringed, then, like the trapped animal that he was and, slowly, his eyes came to rest on the poison bottle in Wentworth's hand.

"This bottle," Wentworth said quietly, "contains white arsenic. It isn't a very pleasant poison to take, and it doesn't kill at once. There is a lot of pain. Agony in the stomach, convulsions, then blood in your mouth...."

The man licked his loose lips, "Now, listen," he said, "you ain't going to make me take nothing like that! Damn you, I ain't afraid of you! You do anything to me and the chief will take care of you. He'll finish you off, just like that!"

"Your chief is a yellow dog like all crooks," Wentworth went on. "Even the police can't get to you here... and the river is just outside the back door. I could have my men hold you and pour this down your throat. I could sit here and watch you die... and then slide your body into the river. Your chief?" Wentworth laughed shortly. "Your chief is a punk."

"My chief is..." The man's face turned crafty. "You wouldn't dare do all that to me," he whined. "And you're just trying to pump me. Well, I ain't talking, see? You can't make me!"

Wentworth lifted his voice. "Ram Singh."

The crook cringed toward the wall as the Sikh's soft step heralded his approach. *"Han, sahib!"*

Wentworth said steadily, "I'm going to poison a rat. Hold him." His gray-blue eyes were merciless, cold, but they were carefully estimating the man before him. He would break all right. As for the contents of the bottle, it was a bitter drug that was poisonous in huge doses, but in smaller quantities would merely cause pains and nausea... Ram Singh was bending over the cot and the broad, keen blade of his knife was laid against the man's throat!

"Open your mouth, rat," said Ram Singh, fiercely, "or I will cut a hole through which to pour this rat poison!"

"No!" the man gasped. "God, no! You can't! The Skull will wipe you out!"

"The Skull is a yellow rat," Wentworth said softly. "Who is the Skull?"

"The Skull is..." The man gagged "The Skull is..." A powerful convulsion shook him and a tinge of blue crept into his pallid cheeks.

An oath jerked from Wentworth's lips. He sprang to a rack of bottles against the wall. He needed no more indication than this. The man was poisoned! Even while his eye raced over the bottles, picking an emetic, his mind flashed to the memory of Donald Beck bending over this unconscious man in the street; of Robert Forbes saying, "I gave him a new restorative to use...."

He whirled back to the cot... and saw that he was already too late. The man was stiffening in death, his face purple with congested blood... his tongue forever stilled! A cold anger flared in Wentworth's eyes, and he spun toward the door of the laboratory where Forbes and Beck were. He could not be sure that either had a hand in this, but both had had the opportunity. He took a long stride toward the door... and a signal bell whirred beside an annunciator there! Wentworth flipped a tumbler. "Yes?"

"Master Richard." It was the quavering voice of old Jenkyns, his butler, who had served Wentworth's father before him. "Master Richard, there are some policemen at the south gate with a search warrant! They insist on coming in! They say there's a dead man here, a *murdered* man!"

CHAPTER 3
MURDER CHARGE

FOR A moment, Wentworth stared in unseeing incredulity at the blank face of the annunciator, then he laughed shortly and a gleam came into his gray-blue eyes—a gleam that might be admiration! The Skull, as the criminal now dead had termed the murder-master, worked with a swift efficiency, and an absolute reliance on his underlings. This meant without doubt that the Skull had ordered this man's death and had been sure enough of the results to tip off the police in advance! Just for that instant while he stared, wordless, Wentworth knew a quickening of his old joy in battle. If there were not such dire results from the operations of this man called "Skull," it would be a pleasure to join issues with such a clever and efficient adversary!

Now....

Wentworth's voice, when he spoke, showed nothing of the inner turmoil the announcement created. "Very well, Jenkyns," he said. "You may admit the police, but go personally to the gate and usher them in. I will receive them in the drawing-room." He turned from the annunciator and threw a single Punjab phrase at Ram Singh. "Hide the body!" His gesture indicated a secret doorway in the wall of the room and then he stepped out into the main laboratory.

He was ready.

Beck was staring intently at Forbes who, a laboratory apron hurriedly donned, was bending over a test-tube which simmered over a Bunsen burner. As Wentworth watched, the tube changed from red to blue and a fine snow of white crystals began to precipitate out in the liquid. Forbes uttered an exclamation of satisfaction.

"You were right, Mr. Wentworth," he cried out. "It's poison all right! Aconitum!"

Wentworth nodded. "I wonder if you gentlemen would accompany me to the drawing-room," he said pleasantly. "The police have a search warrant to serve on me and they will doubtless want to ask some questions."

"A search warrant!" Forbes' eyes widened behind his glasses, then a hint of angry red began to creep into his florid cheeks. "They have a nerve! What do they expect to find here?"

Beck's fists were knotted. "What do you want me to do, sir?" he asked indignantly.

Wentworth shrugged, but his answer was to Forbes as he drew out a cigarette case and preferred it. "From what Jenkyns told me," he said placidly, "they expect to find a murdered man. After you, gentlemen."

Forbes continued to berate the police indignantly as the elevator bore them upward to the third floor drawing-room. Wentworth's eyes were apparently on the slow coiling of smoke that eddied up from his cigarette... but he was watching both the men. Forbes' indignation seemed a little overdone. Beck's face was pale and intent. Wentworth touched his hand and put into it the automatic he had taken from the detective, and Beck's face flushed.

"Thank you, sir," he said. It was plain that he accepted the return of his weapon as indicative of Wentworth's trust. "Will they make trouble about the man we took prisoner?"

Wentworth shrugged. "They may. I'm sorry now that I let him go, but he succeeded in convincing me that he had no connection with the trouble at the drugstore, except to make one of the mob. I couldn't really blame him for that, though the police might."

Forbes said, a little sharply. "Funny we didn't see him go out... Do you want us to forget we saw him?"

Wentworth murmured, "Not in the least... Beck, you said you had a proposition to make to me. I think this will probably be our best opportunity. I shall be pretty busy from now on."

Beck's head jerked toward Wentworth and then a slow smile grew in Beck's eyes. He laughed, "You're the coolest man I've ever seen, sir," he said. "It would be a pleasure to serve you. The proposition...."

THE ELEVATOR door opened and Wentworth ushered

the two men into the drawing-room. Curled up on an end of a davenport, a book in her hands, a girl lifted an alert, small-featured face. She brushed a strand of golden hair back from her forehead.

"I declare, Richard," she called. "You startled me... Why, Mr. Forbes, you didn't go, after all. I'm so glad."

Forbes stammered something not quite intelligible, and despite his inner tension, Wentworth hid a smile. Apparently Melissa Moulin had completed the subjugation of Robert Forbes after Nita and he had left. Wentworth presented Beck briefly.

"A real live detective!" exclaimed Melissa. "Oh, I've always wanted to meet a real detective! Promise me you won't tell Mr. Forbes any of the perfectly horrid things I'm afraid you'll find out about me!"

Beck's smile was quick, "I won't if you'll promise to let me report in private." He promised. "Mr. Wentworth, sir, if you really want me to talk to you now...."

Wentworth nodded, "Go right ahead." Ram Singh had had ample time to dispose of the body, Wentworth thought, listening for the hum of the elevator which would announce the arrival of the police. He was beginning to wish, though, that he had told Ram Singh to slip the body into the river. There was just a chance they would find that hidden doorway....

Melissa was prattling, "Jenkyns told me some policemen were coming here. Isn't it exciting?" Her brown eyes stretched very wide as she looked up trustingly into Forbes' face. "Richard, you won't mind if I stay, will you? I'm sure Cousin Nita won't object at all." Wentworth bowed to her and continued to focus his apparent attention on Beck.

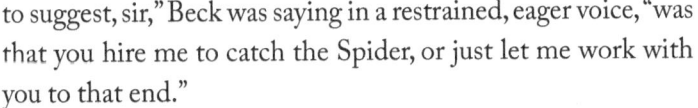

If only he could be sure Nita was safe!

It was strange that she did not at least phone to him… "What I wanted to suggest, sir," Beck was saying in a restrained, eager voice, "was that you hire me to catch the Spider, or just let me work with you to that end."

Wentworth lifted a quizzical eyebrow and his gray-blue eyes swung completely to Beck. His previous suspicions of Beck returned. He had not forgotten that either this man or Forbes had had a chance to poison the prisoner. It was possible, of course, that someone in the mob had done it also. Beck was talking rapidly….

"It's this way, sir," he was saying. "My reasons don't matter particularly, except that you can understand what it would do for my reputation as a private detective. But there is every reason why you should, sir. You've been accused a number of times of being the Spider. You've always disproved the charges and no sensible person ever suspected you. But as long as the Spider is at liberty, you're going to be bothered by these charges. Every time the Spider kills, somebody is going to say, 'It's that criminologist, Wentworth. He's got an in with the police or he'd have been captured long ago.'"

Wentworth smiled. "And you think, Beck, that you can succeed where the police and everyone else has failed?"

"With you to help me! Yes, sir!" Beck was standing up as rigidly as a soldier on parade. Damn it, hard to suspect him of any duplicity, but Wentworth had been deceived before this by his own quick sympathies.

"That's very flattering," Wentworth said, "but I hardly think...."

"You're going to say that you approve of the Spider," Beck cried. "That he accomplishes more in the enforcement of law than all the police. But don't you see that he brings the law into disrepute? He makes the police seem stupid. He damages their morale. He hurts them with the people. And what is the Spider at bottom? A cold-blooded killer! What is that red seal of his but a boast that he has killed? He might as well take their scalps like a savage Indian and cut off their heads for trophies!"

"You don't believe in... killing criminals, Beck?"

"The state provides for their execution, sir, at need. And the Spider—how can he be so sure that he kills only guilty men, as is his boast? Is he God that he alone can tell the guilty from the innocent?"

The challenge and the fire in Donald Beck's eyes shook Wentworth, and the young detective had unwittingly touched on a sore spot. Wentworth was too intelligent not to have realized long ago these very dangers that Beck had cited. He had always been very sure before he called on his swift guns to execute the justice that so often was evaded in the courts... but was he infallible? To his own ears, Wentworth's laughter sounded a little strained.

"Fortunately," he said, "I'm not called upon to pass judgment on the Spider. I think he serves the people and the state better than they deserve, but…."

"Think it over, sir," Beck urged. "Has the Spider ever come forward when you were accused, to free you? You owe yourself and your friends the safety of definite proof that you are not the Spider. As long as any doubt exists… you are not safe. No one that you even love is safe!"

Melissa made her narrow, sloping shoulders shudder delicately. "Oh, you frighten me, Mr. Beck!" she exclaimed. "You must be very brave to be willing to do a thing like that…."

THE DOOR of the elevator opened and Wentworth heard Jenkyns' calm voice ushering in the police. His eyes went searchingly to Melissa, still prattling. Nita had warned him that Melissa was much more than the fluffy, helpless thing she seemed. It looked very much as if she had broken into the conversation to warn him that the elevator was on the way up… Melissa was gracefully on her feet now. She clapped her hands together childishly.

"Oh!" she said. "Real policemen!"

Wentworth pivoted calmly to face the police and a swift frown dented his forehead. There were police all right, but the man who strode at their head, quick and sharp in his movements, stabbing inquisitive glances about him, was not one of the cops. It was the district attorney, Wilton Toley! In contrast to the alertness of his movements, his voice was ponderous, slightly pompous. He prodded each person in the room with his eyes as if he quizzed a stubborn jury.

"Your promptness is very courteous, Mr. Wentworth," he

RICHARD WENTWORTH

said, and there was a flourish like a gesture in his speech. "I have imposed on your good will to start my men searching the lower floors before talking to you."

How soon had that search started? Wentworth wondered sharply. Had Ram Singh had ample time... "Not at all, Mr.

Toley," he said steadily. "I have quite a good deal to tell you, but I wonder if you will allow me to call Commissioner Kirkpatrick first? It would save a great deal of time to tell the story only once, and I fancy I shall be rather busy for a while."

"You may be," Toley murmured. "Yes, indeed. You won't think I'm discourteous, I hope, if I ask you to begin at once? I'm afraid there isn't time to wait for Kirkpatrick."

Wentworth said bluntly, "You refuse to allow me to call Kirkpatrick?"

Toley blinked, imperturbable as a judge, "If you wish to phrase it so."

Melissa tugged at Wentworth's elbow and he felt the mounting tension within him relax a trifle. No mistaking the hostility in Toley's manner, of course. Like all district attorneys, he was out to make a name for himself... and as Beck had pointed out, if the Spider was involved, Wentworth was suspect.

"Melis'," Wentworth said gravely, "I want to present the district attorney of New York County, Wilton Toley. Mr. Toley, this is Miss van Sloan's cousin from New Orleans, Melissa Moulin."

Immediately, Melissa was cooing up at Toley, flattering him.

Toley had difficulty in interrupting long enough to order his men to search the living quarters....

"Oh, good heavens!" Melissa squealed. "You're not going into *my* room! Why, all my... my clothes..." She blushed. "You must allow me to... tidy up a bit!" She ran lightly to the door, her small, white hands fluttering.

Toley cleared his throat, frowned, then waved a hand to the police to let it go. He swung back to Wentworth, "Who is this dead man?" he snapped.

Wentworth smiled slowly. "I was waiting for you to tell me."

Toley took two quick charging steps forward, pointed an admonitory finger at Wentworth. "Don't try to evade my question, Wentworth!"

Wentworth said, "Don't be an ass, Toley! There's no jury here for you to impress."

Toley's face whitened: his voice hoarsened. "We'll find that poor murdered man if we have to tear this building apart! You've been masquerading as a respectable citizen too long!"

Wentworth shrugged. "Provided you personally underwrite the damages, go ahead, Toley." He offered his cigarette case to Beck. "I've been thinking over your proposition, Mr. Beck. Suppose we say—it's a deal?"

"Good!" Beck cried. "The first thing is to inform the newspapers. I'll get on the phone right away."

Toley blocked Beck's path to the door. "There'll be no telephoning until I give the word," he said shortly. "Naturally anyone in this house is suspect. You'll make it easier for yourself if you tell the truth."

Beck grinned at him. "That's what my mother always taught me."

Toley's face grew livid, but his voice came out clear, edged. "You say you were going to telephone the newspapers... Why?"

"I was going to announce," Beck said easily, "that Mr. Wentworth is declaring war on the Spider; that he will not rest until the Spider is brought to justice!"

Toley laughed harshly, "That's a laugh," he said. "Why, of all the effrontery. Wentworth is...."

"Be careful of what you say, Toley," Wentworth interrupted easily. "I have witnesses. There is such a thing as criminal libel."

Toley swung toward him, but what he was about to say was never uttered. A policeman slammed out of the elevator and came forward at a run. His face was red with excitement.

"Mr. Toley," he panted. "They... they found the body! *And he's got the Spider's seal on him!*"

CHAPTER 4
THE SPIDER WALKS AGAIN

TRIUMPH WAS almost a smirk on the face of Wilton Toley as he whirled once more to confront Wentworth. He drew himself up to his full brief height and Wentworth could see, almost visibly, the formal words of arrest taking shape in the man's brain. Something like desperation was goading Wentworth. He had been mad to conceal the body in the first place, but he had wanted only to avoid the delay which police investigation would entail—to prevent the embarrassment of such a discovery to his friend, Kirkpatrick, the commissioner of police.

What Donald Beck had said was all too true, that each time he managed to turn aside the charges which were leveled at him, Kirkpatrick's enemies made capital of it. But this seal of the Spider? How in the name of heaven had that come to be placed on the body? More of the Skull's work, without a doubt. The man was damnably clever....

"Richard Wentworth," Toley was drawing the full drama from the situation."I place you under arrest on a charge of...."

The new opening of the elevator door cut him short and a tall man, as precise in his dress as a marine officer, stepped crisply forward—Stanley Kirkpatrick, the commissioner.

"I got your message, Dick," he said easily. "It just happened I was around the corner at the scene of that gangster raid and so I came right away. I understood it was important."

Toley glared at Wentworth. "My orders were disobeyed!" he said harshly. "That girl...."

From the doorway, Melissa Moulin ran forward. "Oh, did I do wrong, Mr. Toley?" she asked anxiously. "I didn't know. You said there wasn't time, or that was what I thought. So after I finished straightening up my room, I just called up the police. I was sure Mr. Kirkpatrick would come quickly, and...."

Toley swore harshly and Melissa put a shocked expression on her tiny face, threw back her head. "Mr. Toley!" she exclaimed.

"Down home a man would be horsewhipped for using language like that in the presence of ladies!"

There was a grim smile on Wentworth's lips that had its echo on the saturnine face of Commissioner Kirkpatrick. Wentworth took advantage of the diversion to speak in a low voice to Donald Beck. "If you escape arrest," he said quietly, "stay here on guard. If Miss van Sloan comes back here, tell her exactly what happened, please, and take orders from her."

Toley threw his hands into the air in token of surrender as Melissa turned an indignant back on his protestations. Wentworth was grateful for Kirkpatrick's presence but it did complicate matters. If Toley persisted in his present course, Wentworth would have no alternative except flight. He would use that only as a last resort. It crippled him damnably to have to dodge policemen while he was working on a case and he knew, without question, that the coming struggle with the Skull would tax his resources to the utmost!

"Kirkpatrick," Toley said abruptly, "I was attempting to handle this case without interference...."

"And usurping my privileges!" Kirkpatrick took instant fire from the other's manner. "May I remind you once more, Mr. District Attorney, that it is my duty to gather evidence, yours to present it to juries for prosecution?"

"Exactly," Toley purred. "But when you neglect that duty, Mr. Commissioner, I may find it necessary to present other charges before the jury... concerning you!"

The pointed ends of Kirkpatrick's black mustache bristled. "Be careful, Toley!"

"Take that advice for yourself," Toley snapped. "I demand that you arrest Wentworth for murder!"

"Are you swearing out the warrant, Toley?"

Wentworth lounged against the wall, but he had estimated every man in the room. Forbes stood with Melissa near the French doors to the terrace. At the hall exit was a single policeman whom Wentworth could reach in two bounds. Beyond that... but he did not know how other officers were distributed about the place. It made escape damnably difficult.

Toley said violently, "Yes, I'll swear out the warrant!"

Kirkpatrick shrugged, "In that case, the responsibility is on your shoulders, and I won't have to face a suit for false arrest. Dick...."

Wentworth drew in a slow breath. This was painful. It would besmirch Kirkpatrick's record if he made his escape, but there seemed no other course....

Toley was watching them keenly. "Better draw your gun, Commissioner," he said, happily. "He's a dangerous man! We just found the man he murdered here in his own house... with the Spider seal on him!"

WENTWORTH SAW Kirkpatrick's face tighten with pain and it wrung his heart. They were fast friends, he and Kirkpatrick, but the commissioner would never swerve from his duty by so much as the breadth of a knife-edge. He had long been convinced that Wentworth was the Spider, and had warned him that if ever the evidence fell into his hands, he would prosecute to the full extent of the law!

Wentworth respected his rigorous attention to duty—and so made sure that the evidence was never gathered! Meantime, as Richard Wentworth, he had often helped Kirkpatrick in his battles against the underworld... Kirkpatrick was bracing himself to perform his duty. Wentworth sucked in a slow breath, gathered his energies for the dash he must make....

The policeman at the door spoke. "Maybe, Mr. Toley, you better hear about this business first, sir," he said. "Maybe I didn't tell it to you quite straight."

Toley whirled toward the policeman. "What do you mean, dolt?"

The officer reddened, "I don't have to take that off you, Mr. Toley," he said. "You ain't my boss, and even off the commissioner...."

"Tell your story, Finnegan," Kirkpatrick interrupted. "Toley, keep a civil tongue between your teeth."

The policeman grinned slightly. "Yes, Commissioner. It's like this. We found this body floating in the river...."

Wentworth felt relief like a fierce laughter pumping at his chest, but he managed to appear indifferent. He tapped a cigarette.

Patrolman Finnegan was still talking. "He had this Spider seal between his shoulders, and...."

"That's proof enough," Toley snapped. "We've got witnesses who saw Wentworth carrying the man into this place. They'll identify him, and...."

"Identification ain't going to be so easy," Finnegan said, and there was a gleam of hard amusement in his eye. "This body didn't have no clothes on, and likewise it didn't have no fingers or no head. It looks like maybe he had some tattooing on his chest, but if he did, he ain't now. His chest was skinned."

With an angry exclamation, Forbes batted open the terrace doors and led Melissa outside; she seemed suddenly faint. Wentworth stared with a sick amazement at Finnegan. Such ghastly mutilation… But this was impossible! It couldn't be the man who had died of poison in his laboratory. God, to treat a human being like that… He felt the weight of Kirkpatrick's shocked stare and his head swung slowly to meet his friend's gaze. There was a pinched pain in Kirkpatrick's eyes and an awful doubt… Believing as he did that Wentworth was the Spider, he must blame him for this, even though there was no proof!

"You say," Kirkpatrick asked the police officer heavily, "that this man had a Spider seal between his shoulders?"

Wentworth wanted fiercely to deny that he was responsible but anything he could say would be an admission that he was the Spider.…

Beck jerked eagerly at his elbow. "You see, sir," Beck cried, "I told you the Spider was nothing but a cold-blooded killer! By God, I'll work day and night to catch him! With your help, sir, well succeed!"

Kirkpatrick swung his head sharply toward Toley, and there was a grimness along his set jaw that Wentworth recognized. When that drawn look came to Kirkpatrick's face, it meant that he had determined upon a course that hurt him to the heart—

but it also meant that he would carry through, unswervingly, to the end!

"Who are your witnesses, Toley?" he asked harshly.

"Wait, Kirk," Wentworth pushed out words with difficulty. "Wait just a moment… Beck, you may phone the papers if Mr. Toley no longer objects. I cannot believe that the Spider would do such a thing as this, but I have no choice. I pledge myself to track down the Spider… *If the Spider is guilty, he shall pay!*"

Kirkpatrick's eyes were burning into his, and slowly the tension went out of the commissioner's saturnine face. He dragged a heavy hand down across his cheeks. "Yes, yes," he said slowly, "it is hard to believe the Spider would do a thing like that."

Toley had been watching them closely, and there was a secretive light in his eyes. Wentworth wondered if he had grasped the significance of Kirkpatrick's indignation and the reason for its abrupt termination. Kirkpatrick was not good at dissembling….

Toley's voice was purring, soft. "I withdraw my charges against Wentworth, Commissioner," he said. "Even if he were the Spider—*and* I'll admit I have no proof of it now—I can't believe that any civilized human being would perform such mutilation."

"Please, sir." The officer, Finnegan, stepped into the room. "The medical examiner was there when the body was hauled out of the water. He said it looked like a case of aconitum poisoning. He said that the mutilation had been done after death."

The tautness that had left Wentworth began to creep back again. He whispered a name in his mind, *Ram Singh*. In God's name, what had he pledged himself with his promise to track down the Spider! He began to talk rapidly, telling of the raid on the drugstore and the things that had happened there; of the test Forbes had run in his basement laboratory which had revealed aconitum in the Aspo-Seltzer.

"We should talk to that druggist," Wentworth said finally, "and certainly Wister should be interviewed as president of the concern that shipped out the poisoned drug. I don't for a moment suspect him of poisoning his own drugs, but it should certainly be investigated."

Kirkpatrick nodded stiffly, "This is the third case of drug poisoning that has developed in the city tonight," he said. "There have been seven other deaths, besides those you know of, Dick! In each case Wister's products have been responsible!"

"Good Lord!" Wentworth whispered. "Eleven human beings killed in a single night by the poison alone! What madman can be behind this? What can he hope to gain?"

The fury that had always shaken him at the wanton slaughter of the innocent took cold possession of his soul. He had hoped that he had discovered this new conspiracy of murder at its first stages; that he could check its spread at once. The Spider was already too late for that, but there must be no further delay. He must run down at once the few leads he possessed....

District Attorney Toley was speaking excitedly. "I'll admit we should interview Wister," he said sharply, his face pale, "but we can't get a man of his importance out of bed at this time of night—especially since he can't have anything active to do with it. My God, what a case! When this gets to court...."

Wentworth felt contempt for Toley stir within him. In the midst of such encroaching horror, Toley could think only about his own reputation as a prosecutor; about disturbing Wister! Wentworth did not protest. It accorded with his plans that Wister should not be disturbed—by the police. It would give the Spider time to pay a call!

"It would be too bad to disturb Wister," he said dryly, "but may I suggest that, as a preventive measure, you should prohibit any further shipment of drugs from his concern until they can be inspected for poison?"

Kirkpatrick swung toward Wentworth. "That, certainly, will be done. I'll have men there before the plant opens in the morning. About the druggist... I've already sent men to his home. Nothing more will be allowed to go out of that store or any other to which poison has been traced. Every store in the city must make a check-up at once. By the way, Dick, I should have mentioned this before. Was Jackson doing any work for you? He was knocked out by the blast at that drugstore, and has been sent to Medical Center. A slight concussion is all, I believe...."

THE BUZZ of the telephone cut in on his words and Jenkyns appeared in the doorway, rigid with resentment of the police intrusion; his head with its silvery cap of hair carried high. "For Mr. Kirkpatrick, sir," he reported.

Wentworth signed to him to bring in a portable phone while his thoughts raced with the implication of Jackson's injury. He must phone the hospital... He had hoped that Jackson was with Nita, protecting her! He must get rid of these men, and hurry into battle… His head jerked toward Kirkpatrick, who was handing back the phone to Jenkyns.

"The druggist hasn't reached home yet," he said. "You understood that Nita had left with him?"

Wentworth felt apprehension tauten the leaders of his throat, squeeze his heart like a cold hand. God! What had happened to Nita! Those killers of the Skull had thrown a bomb which obviously was intended to kill the owner of the store. Had they… had they renewed their attack? Had they seized Nita or… or worse? Jerkily, he voiced his apprehensions and Kirkpatrick echoed them, put out an immediate general alarm for both Nita and the druggist.

"There's no more that can be done now," he said. "I'll let you know as soon as I hear anything."

Wentworth thanked him heavily. His hands were working into knotted fists at his side, remembering the sweetness of Nita's laughter in the spring dusk. "No alarm is going to ring in *your* district tonight," she had said. No alarm!

"If you'll excuse me," he said thickly, "I think…."

Toley seemed on fire to get away and Kirkpatrick crossed to put his hand warmly on Wentworth's shoulder. "Don't worry, old man," he said. "Nita was probably afraid some attack would be made on the druggist and is taking him to a place of safety. We'll hear from her soon."

Wentworth nodded, with an attempt at casualness. "Of course," he agreed quietly, but apprehension gnawed at his heart. What more could he do than the police were already attempting? A city-wide alarm with thousands of men on the lookout…

No, the Spider could add little to that, even if his stern sense of duty would permit him to turn aside from the trail of the Skull. He could only hope that he could find the man responsible for these massacres—in time... In time? With eleven already dead? Wentworth strangled a sharp, sardonic laughter. It was already too late, much too late....

Forbes was leaving, too, but Beck would remain in accordance with Wentworth's orders. Wentworth moved blindly toward the terrace, found Melissa there and told her swiftly of his fears for Nita.

"I must leave the house shortly in an attempt to find her," he said. "I'll leave Jenkyns here and this man, Beck, on guard. I'm not sure that Beck is reliable. Find out for me, Melissa."

The girl's dainty face turned up to his and there was no coquetry at all in her gaze. "I'll do my best, Richard," she said.

A faint smile touched Wentworth's lips. "I fancy that will be adequate," he said. "I haven't thanked you for calling Kirkpatrick, but you have my sincere admiration. It was neatly done."

Melissa lifted a shoulder, slightly, "Self-important men are always so easy," she murmured. "Good-night, Richard..." She ran toward the French doors, paused just outside. "Oh, Mr. Beck, Richard says that you're going to protect poor little me"

There was laughter in Beck's answer. "Melissa, I'm the one that needs protection, with you around."

WENTWORTH'S FACE was lifted tautly toward the tender sky. He whispered, *Nita!* A tremor ran through his body and his face was twisted, almost ugly, with a relaxation of control that this grimly powerful man rarely allowed even when alone. It lasted only a moment, then his face was wiped bare of expression.

He swung about and paced with an easy deceptive swiftness toward another door that gave into his private suite. He did not stop there but went into the music room which adjoined his sleeping-chamber and strode toward a pipe organ that filled one end of the room.

Standing where he could reach the orifices of the treble pipes, he beat on them in a soft, irregular rhythm with his palms so that a ghost of melody came forth. Then he strode toward a near-by wall panel and, as he reached it, the panel slid aside and he stepped through into a compact dressing-room. He jabbed a bell-button in the wall and threw himself down before a brightly illuminated make-up mirror. His hands went deftly, instantly, to work.

A pungent liquid from a bottle tautened the skin of his face until it stretched tightly over the bones and turned sallow. A few deft touches wiped out his lips and changed his mouth into a straight gash; his nose, altered with putty, became a predatory beak. He was putting the finishing touches on that part of his disguise when a door opposite the one by which he had entered, slid open. Ram Singh stepped through. He salaamed even lower than usual, and there was apprehension in his devoted gaze.

"*Wah, Sahib,*" he said, his deep voice subdued to a murmur. "It was filthy work, but it had to be done. I found upon the rat's chest a duplicate of your own seal, master! I knew then that someone plotted against thee; that it was meant for this dead thing to be found. I… did what was necessary to keep him from being identified."

Wentworth was adjusting heavy false brows over his own, patting them exactly into place with touches of his lean, competent fingers. The Sikh flung himself to his knees and ripped his knife from its sheath, set its point against his breast.

"If I have done wrong, master," he cried, "thy servant knows how to die!"

Wentworth turned slowly from the mirror and there was a gentleness in his eyes that few men had ever seen there. He said, quietly, "Thou are my child and my brother, oh warrior of the Sikhs. Who shall question what one friend does for another?" He reached out his hand and touched the hilt of the great-bladed knife. "Thy arms are without stain, thou Singh."

Ram Singh bounded to his feet and pride flashed in his eyes again. "My master has made me whole again," he said simply. "I put dynamite in the head, and that and the rest I blew to bits in the river. It was a demolition charge, *sahib.*" His eyes squinted in disgust. "*Wah!* What a job for a warrior!"

Wentworth smiled faintly as he turned back to the mirror, and the things he had done to his face made that smile a menacing thing. He could not censure the Sikh… but he had made a promise that if the Spider were responsible—the Spider should pay! Grimly, he drew a lank black wig over his head and, from the mirror there stared back at him… the ominous face of the Spider!

"We shall want the Daimler, Ram Singh," Wentworth said quietly. "We go secretly, if possible. To Bayside."

Moments later, a long black cape draped over artificially hunched shoulders, a wide-brimmed hat concealing half his face, Wentworth sped downward by a secret stairway and found Ram Singh waiting in a cross-tunnel buried deep beneath the basement. Through it, they moved without words for a considerable distance before they entered a narrow elevator that lofted them rapidly into a private garage. The doors opened at the wink of the headlights and the heavy, sleek car of the Spider rolled out into the street and whirled swiftly northward.

THE ILLUMINATED dial of Wentworth's watch showed three o'clock, but the slums which jostled against wealthy Sutton Place were strangely alive. Windows showed the glow of lights and once when traffic lights stopped him, Wentworth saw a group of men about a tenement doorway where an ambulance stood. They were close together, silent, and there was a tension, almost fright in the way they huddled there, waiting. Already, the poisonings were laying their weight of terror upon the people.

While Wentworth's car stood motionless, waiting through the slow seconds for the light to change, he caught the hoarse wail of another ambulance siren. Death. Dead and dying everywhere… In the name of heaven, what could be the motive behind the wanton slaughter of these innocents?

For a moment, Wentworth hesitated… but what could he accomplish here? Once the poison had been administered, only doctors and the hospitals could help. His was a grimmer task—to find the men behind this horror and wipe them out! The gleam in the Spider's eyes was cold as death itself.

Wentworth's mind flashed back to the youthful Donald Beck

and his indignation against the Spider—"a cold-blooded killer." Perhaps… but what was the Skull? How else could such criminals be answered than with the weapons they, themselves, elected to use? No one suffered more than Wentworth himself from the course he was forced to follow. He had his own moments of bleak questioning and self-doubt….

A wail that Wentworth at first mistook for the distant shriek of a thinner siren jerked at his consciousness and Wentworth stared fixedly at the dark streets through which the car whirled so effortlessly. That wail had a curiously human tone, and….

Abruptly, Wentworth rapped on the glass behind Ram Singh, and the Daimler snubbed to a halt. At the same moment, Wentworth flung himself to the street. He had found the origin of that haunting sound. A woman ran along the street, desperately crying for help, staggering with a child heavy and inert in her arms….

"This way," Wentworth called sharply. "This way, I'll get you to the hospital."

The woman swerved toward him, stretching out the child toward him. "Oh, help me," she cried. "My baby! My little baby…" Her face was twisted with the strain of inward pain, of her violent exertion, and her eyes were frantic. Pale hair streamed back from her temples. She wore only a threadbare coat over a nightgown and her feet were bare, were bleeding. "Oh, help my baby!"

Wentworth caught the child from her arms and flung himself into the tonneau after the woman. "The hospital, quickly," he snapped. He jerked up a kick-seat and laid the child across it, bent swiftly to feel the pulse, flicked back an eye-lid; whipped open a compartment from which he drew a first-aid kit.

The Daimler was surging across town now, racing for a hospital. Ram Singh's deep voice came back to Wentworth's ears. The Sikh was speaking in Punjabi. "Master, hast thou forgotten? Thou wearest the garb of the Spider!"

He sent Wister backward across the room
until he crashed against a work bench.

Wentworth's lips grew thin against his teeth as he worked over the child. Adrenalin for that laboring heart; an antidote for the swift poison which he believed he had identified... No, he had not forgotten that he wore the disguise of the Spider; nor that he might be identified as Richard Wentworth through this car. He had not forgotten, but if he could save this one life....

Beside him, the woman's voice ran on endlessly, "Oh, I don't understand," she was whispering. "Mary wasn't very sick—not terribly ill. Just a heavy cold, and the doctor said she'd be all right in a few days. He gave me some medicine. But now...."

WENTWORTH SWORE under his breath. So the pollution of poison had reached even into the offices of doctors! It was damnable, fiendish—this sly death that sneaked into the homes of the sick. Where could they turn, these ailing and stricken ones, if the very healing potions turned to murder in their bodies? This child's pale, blue-tinged face, the dark smudges of shadow beneath the closed eyes, burned its way into his brain. Donald Beck should have been with him now....

A quiver ran over the child's frail body, and a faint stirring. The eyes fluttered open and Wentworth caught the breath of a sound from the pale lips. "Mother..." A great relief surged over Wentworth and he realized how tautly he had bent over the child. He smiled and turned toward the mother.

"I think your baby will be all right now," he said quietly. "Only, there must be no more strain on that heart. Absolute quiet... Tell them at the hospital that I gave her..." He detailed the treatment while the woman bent over the child, and drew it into her lap. There was the wet glisten of tears on her cheeks when she looked up.

"You saved my baby," she whispered. "You…" Her eyes widened suddenly, and she shrank back in the corner of the cushions… and Wentworth realized that he had been smiling, and in the Spider disguise, that made his face an awful thing.

He said, gently, "You have nothing to fear from me."

An uncertain smile touched the woman's lips. "No, of course not. You… you saved my baby. You… That black cape, your face. I know you now. You are the Spider. You are a great man!" The car slid to a quiet halt at the emergency entrance of the hospital.

"I won't go in," Wentworth told the woman. "Just tell them what I did and they'll take care of your baby." He swung open the door, stepped to the ground to help her down.

The woman's hand clutched his. "You saved my baby, Mr. Spider!" she said. "I…."

Before Wentworth guessed her intention, the woman had bowed her head and pressed a kiss upon the back of his hand. He felt the wetness of her falling tears, then she was running toward the hospital door. He stood there, motionless, staring after her, and his fingers touched wonderingly the spot where she had kissed. There was a straining tightness in his own throat… and the light of the opening door reached out into the darkness and fell across him. There was a nurse there and behind her the blue of a policeman's uniform.

For the moment, Wentworth forgot his dress, forgot that the light that flung out through the doorway was brilliant and struck across him like a spotlight. He forgot it until he heard the policeman's cry, and saw him spring forward with a hand fumbling for his gun.

"The Spider!" the policeman shouted. "The Spider! Halt, or I'll fire!"

With a wrench, Wentworth flung himself into the car and at the same moment Ram Singh hurled it forward into the darkness. Behind them, the policeman's gun poked fiery holes into the night. Once, a bullet clanged off the armored body of the Daimler, then it was gone....

Wentworth settled back against the cushion—with a slow breath of released tension. There might be-pursuit, but the Spider would not turn aside from his mission of vengeance, of death perhaps. His fingers touched once more the spot that a mother's lips had pressed in gratitude.

CHAPTER 5
THE FLESHLESS ONES

IT WAS almost four o'clock when the Daimler, with throttled motor, rolled through the dark and deserted streets of Bayside and approached the waterside estate of Samuel Wister, head of the Eastern Drug Corporation—whose medicaments had spread poison death through the city this night. In spite of the lateness of the hour, lights shone in the huge brick pile of Wister's home—one on the second floor and others in a low wing that stretched out toward the water.

So much Wentworth discovered before he and Ram Singh parked the Daimler in the shrubbery-choked driveway of a nearby untenanted house. It was a wild-seeming section to be found within the limits of New York City. Wister's home itself was shielded from the road both by a high thick wall and by close-planted shrubbery which had grown to the proportion of trees. It was possible to catch only glimpses of the house itself, set well back toward the water.

Through the cover of those trees, their shadows emphasized by the cold, lone moon that floated overhead, the black-caped figure of the Spider flitted as silently as the creature whose name he bore. His goal was that low wing where he expected to find Wister's home laboratory, but first he made a slow circuit of the grounds.

Hard to believe that Wister could be the criminal, less because of any knowledge that Wentworth had of the man himself than because it would seem madness to distribute the poison through his own concern. Nevertheless, the man might know something. There had to be a *reason* for this slaughter... reasons which Toley or Kirkpatrick might not be able to extract. Usually, men told the truth to the Spider. Wentworth's disguised lips cracked in a mirthless smile... The reputation he carried had its advantages, too.

Wentworth completed his circuit of the grounds and, with quiet swiftness, headed for the lighted wing of the Wister home. He was within a hundred feet of it when a sound among the trees ahead froze him into a motionless shadow. He drew the black cape up before his face to hide the loom of its whiteness and his eyes, fully accustomed to the darkness, gradually made out the silhouette of a man who leaned against a tree bole not twenty feet ahead. Even as Wentworth spotted him, the man began to creep toward the house!

After a moment's hesitation, Wentworth followed. The man's every movement suggested the criminal, but had he come to attack—or to consult with Wister? Plainly, robbery was not his purpose, for he went straight toward the lighted portion of the building! Wentworth's hand slid beneath his cape to loosen a heavy automatic in its holster.

Minutes dragged past before Wentworth saw that the man was crouched just beneath a window from which light streamed. If he intended murder... but there was no glint of a weapon in his hand. Tensely, the Spider watched the man dart aside from the window toward a door that opened into the laboratory wing.

When the man touched that door, Wentworth was not ten feet away, crouched in a clump of spirea, whose white flowers were just budding into fragrance. The sweetness of their scent made the whole thing painfully unreal. Furtive shadows moving in the night—perhaps the even grimmer shadow of Death nearby—and in the city he had left men and children dying; but here, the moon poured down its silver and the bridal wreath was fragrant... Wentworth saw that the door was swinging open softly....

WHEN THE slow space of a minute had gone, Wentworth followed through that doorway and paused just inside. Even his keen eyes could see nothing in the black hallway, but he caught faint music from a radio and then the slightest creak of a floor-board. He held his breath and presently there was another creak—farther away. Once more, he slipped forward… then flattened against a wall as light blazed through an open door.

"Howdy, boss," a man's voice was drawling, thin with mockery. "So you thought I wouldn't find you, did you? Thought you were too smart, and…."

The closing door pinched off the words utterly and Wentworth realized that the room into which the man had passed must be sound-proofed. A half dozen long strides took him to the door, but the voices beyond were only a murmur above the muted sound of the radio.

A fierce, cold gleam was in the Spider's eyes. Those few words sounded suspiciously like this was some underling from whom Wister had attempted to hide. There was not necessarily a criminal implication there; not necessarily… His hand closed on the doorknob and he pressed lightly on the portal. Wister's voice came through sharply.

"If you don't get out of here in precisely ten seconds," Wister said coldly, "I'll shoot. There's a gun in my pocket and I can shoot accurately even through the cloth."

"Aw, now, boss," the man was wheedling, "you don't want to get tough with me. *Damn you, I'll….*"

There was the double, muffled beat of gunfire and Wentworth flung wide the door, went half across the room in a bound. The man he had followed was huddled inertly against the wall where bullets had flung him and above the body bent a heavy-shouldered, dynamic man with a gun knotted in his fist with a quick twist; Wentworth took the gun and sent Wister staggering across the room. He brought up against a high work-bench.

"Just take it easy," Wentworth ordered softly, "and it may be that nothing will happen to you. It may be...."

Wister's face was solid-boned above a heavy jaw and his eyes, pale in a darkly tanned face, were narrowed with anger. "You'd have done better to attack together," he said harshly. "*He's* gone to his Maker at any rate."

Wentworth needed no examination of the fallen man to confirm Wister. To a man who has witnessed death many times; there is something unmistakable in the flaccid inertia of a corpse. He smiled bleakly, and his gaze was cold, inflexible. Though he made no movement toward Wister, his voice was flat with menace.

"You may justify this killing," he said, "though the reason the man came here wants some explanation. Wister, in Manhattan tonight, a score of people died from your company's poisoned medicines. *Why*, Wister?"

Wister dragged a heavy hand across his face, dropped into a swivel chair. "God knows," he said dully. "It's ghastly. I've ordered the plant closed pending a check on all supplies." He sat with slumped shoulders; his big, squarish head with its rumpled dark hair was sagging. "You're this man who calls himself the Spider, aren't you?"

Wentworth made no answer. Keeping his eyes on Wister warily, he crouched beside the dead man and presently his groping hands found the thing he had expected. He tossed into Wister's lap a tiny wooden skeleton with grotesquely jiggling arms and legs... the talisman of the Skull!

"A criminal is killing those people for some greedy purpose,

Wister," he said sharply. "This man is his hireling, as the talisman proves. And Wister... *this man called you 'boss.' "*

Wister's head snapped up, "Why damn you! You're implying that I... that I poisoned those poor people!" He lurched to his feet.

Wentworth stood quietly facing him. There was no weapon in his hand. "I'm still asking," he said softly. "If I were sure, Wister, you would not still be answering questions. You would be dead with a small red spider on your forehead!"

Wister's dark face paled a little, but his angry eyes did not falter. For seconds, he held that stiff pose then, as if that brief concentration had tired him unutterably, he sagged back into the chair. "I'm long past the age when bogey-men or masqueraders frighten me," he said thickly. "You can do what you damned please. I'm making no explanations to you." He covered his face with his hands.

A knife-frown dented Wentworth's forehead. There was something peculiar here, but certainly Wister's conduct was not that of a guilty man. Wister knew that, proved guilty, he faced swift retribution at the hands of the Spider, yet he had shown small evidences of fright....

A flash of bright light across the window jerked Wentworth's head that way and a startled oath leaped to his lips. He knew that long black limousine gliding to a halt at the main entrance of the mansion. It was Commissioner Kirkpatrick's car! Wentworth backed toward the door.

"I leave you to the police," he said curtly. "I'd advise you to be more precise in your explanations with them...."

Wister's head snapped up. "The police must not come here," he cried. "They must not. I'll see them in the morning, at my office, but they can't come here...."

Wentworth had his hand on the door and once more the puzzled light crept into his clear eyes. Wister, who did not fear the deadly vengeance of the Spider, was terrified at the approach of the police! It didn't make sense. No time to think of that now. Wister was suddenly snatching at a drawer of his bench. It was laboriously slow, and Wentworth could have whipped out an automatic and fired with deadly accuracy long before the drawer was even opened. But the Spider did not harm innocent men... and until he knew definitely otherwise, Wister must fall in that category.

Wentworth laughed flatly, mockingly, and whipped open the door. As he ducked through, his hand flicked to a leather tool-kit he wore in a girdle about his waist. When he slammed the door shut, it was upon a steel wedge with reticulated teeth on its sloping surfaces. Nothing less than a hydraulic jack would open the door now! The blast of Wister's gun came faintly to his ears through the heavy portal, and a splinter of light stabbed out through the bullet-hole in the door.

An instant later, the Spider slipped out into the moonlit yard. He could see Kirkpatrick's tall figure crossing toward the entrance of the house, following by the bobbing shorter silhouette of District Attorney Toley. Wentworth ducked into the protecting shrubbery and flung himself into a silent sprint toward the nearby driveway where his car was parked. But he was not fleeing; nor was he through yet with Samuel Wister!

When he dropped over the high, thick-built stone wall, the Spider fairly threw himself into the car.

"Get away fast, but silently, Ram Singh," he cried softly to the Sikh. "Allow me ten minutes, then drive into Wister's place… the front door this time, Ram Singh!"

WHEN, PRECISELY ten minutes later, the Daimler drew to a halt behind the police car, an entirely different figure from the hunched, be-caped Spider ran lightly up the main steps of Wister's home. Richard Wentworth was now impeccably dressed in dark tweeds, a light topcoat and soft felt—and his face showed no trace, other than a slight redness, of the recent make-up.

It was a perilous thing he did, in thus again so soon confronting Wister. There might be some trick of voice, some unconscious resemblance that would betray him to the man as the same ominous figure that had recently confronted him in the laboratory. It was a thing Wentworth must risk. The mystery which surrounded Wister would have to be pierced at once… Kirkpatrick's driver was crouched before the dashboard of the car, tinkering with the two-way radio. Damnation! Disablement of the set could be serious at a time like this!

Wentworth punched the bell and, within a few moments, a butler with a heavy, sleep-mottled face, opened the door. Wentworth heard Kirkpatrick's crisp tones and Wister's blustering answers.

"What name, sir?" the butler asked heavily. "Pardon me, sir, is there any word of Miss Nona?"

Wentworth's keen eyes searched the butler's face. "I know of none," he said softly. "Has there been any further message?"

The butler shook his head gravely, took Wentworth's card. "God help Miss Nona, then—begging your pardon, sir."

Wentworth's eyes were half-closed in speculation. Those few words with the butler had given him the clue to Wister's hostility toward the police, and his terror at their arrival... He strolled into the drawing-room, smiling at Toley's angry glare; nodding to Kirkpatrick's quizzical regard. His eyes went past them to Wister's angry, puzzled face.

"I must apologize for this intrusion, Mr. Wister," he said formally. "We belong to some of the same clubs, I believe. Unfortunately we haven't met."

Toley took two choppy strides toward him, "Confound your interfering impertinence," he rasped. "You will leave at once."

Wentworth's eyes were resting on a portrait of a lovely dark-haired girl which hung above the fireplace. "Is that Nona, Wister?" he asked quietly, ignoring Toley. "May I suggest, Wister, that you are being foolish to forego the help of the police at a time like this? Especially since they are already here... and hence, the damage is done."

Wister's pale eyes strained wide. Kirkpatrick's gaze was keen as it flashed from the portrait to Wister and back to Wentworth. Toley was merely bewildered. He continued to rant.

"I suppose you don't know, Wentworth, that the Spider has already called on Mr. Wister!" he snapped.

Wentworth started, made his face angry. "Ahead of me again,

is he? Confound the fellow… but that will have to wait. Will you tell them, Wister, or shall I?"

WISTER LIFTED his heavy shoulders, "I suppose this was inevitable. I don't know how you found out, but… it's true! My ward, Nona Malvern, was kidnapped two days ago! I was afraid to communicate with you, Commissioner, because of the threats that were made. They were asking two hundred thousand dollars ransom and they were supposed to communicate tonight. I… haven't heard yet. That man I killed… At first, I thought he came from them, but apparently not. He was a former employee I had to fire for petty thievery. He had made threats against my life, and then…."

From the door, the butler spoke excitedly, "it's come, sir," he cried. "That man is on the phone, and…."

Wister bolted into a library that opened off the drawing-room, snatched up a telephone. In two strides, Wentworth reached the butler. "The other phone!" he rasped. "Where is it?"

The butler pointed toward a service door in the rear of the hall and Wentworth bounded to it, caught up the instrument.

"I'll pay!" Wister was crying. "I had nothing to do with the police coming here! It's because of the poisonings, I tell you, and—"

A rasping voice cut him short, "That's too bad, Wister. Too damned bad! We warned you. I'm warning you once more. Keep your mouth shut… *You still have a wife, Wister!*"

Wister was still shouting incoherently when the wire went dead. At the click of final disconnection, Wentworth rapidly signaled the operator to have the call traced. Not that he had much hope of success. Criminals knew too much about such matters nowadays; for instance that a call from a dial instrument could not be traced once the connection was broken… He turned away to find Kirkpatrick beside him. Rapidly, he related what he had heard.

Kirkpatrick nodded. "Do you think there's any tie-up between this and the poisonings? I'll admit I can't see it, and Wister will close up tighter than a clam, now. Wait, Dick… Before we go back into the drawing-room. I have some bad news for you."

Wentworth felt his heart tighten. *"Nita!"* he breathed. "For God's sake, Kirk, out with it. Is she…."

"She's alive, and unhurt, Dick, but… that druggist was found dead of poisoning in her apartment. He was phoning when he was stricken and the operator called the police. Toley insisted that we arrest Nita. The charge is… *murder!*"

For a moment, Wentworth stared incredulously at Kirkpatrick, but the relief at news of Nita's safety was so great that laughter curved his mouth corners.

"That's ridiculous," he said quietly. "Toley can't hold Nita on any such trumped-up business as that. That druggist either committed suicide, or some poison took delayed effect on him in Nita's apartment—some more machinations of the man who is behind all these poisonings."

"I'm inclined to agree with you, Dick," Kirkpatrick nodded soberly. "How did you get wind of this kidnapping?"

Wentworth, frowning, had to drive his mind back to the immediate problem. Absently, he told of the butler's question.

"It was a guess," he acknowledged, "but Wister was scarcely

in a position to be so belligerent toward the police, with all those poisonings stemming from his plant—and there was the added fact that he was awake and dressed… Obviously waiting for something. Your driver told me that you had just arrived."

"I hope that will satisfy Toley," Kirkpatrick nodded crisply.

Wentworth was a passive listener while Toley hurled questions at the obviously distracted Wister. There was little else to be learned except the details of the kidnapping… Nona Malvern had been seized from her own roadster just after a brief sail on the bay. The telephoned ransom message had been received before Wister knew that Nona had been taken… Wister did not accompany them to the door as they left and, on the verandah, Wentworth accosted Toley.

"I'm warning you, Toley," he said, with quiet force. "Either dismiss your ridiculous charges against Miss van Sloan at once, or you'll face a damage suit that will drive you out of office! You understand me, I think."

Toley's laughter was sharp as a terrier's bark. "You may get away with murder where the police are concerned," he said, raspingly, "but you can't intimidate my office! Your lawless behavior and that of your woman…."

Wentworth took a single stride forward and there was a blaze in his eyes that sent Toley stumbling backward, pawing awkwardly at his pocket for a gun.

"You will apologize, Toley," Wentworth said; his voice dead level.

Toley had the gun out and his voice lifted shrilly. "You take one more step forward and I'll by God shoot you down!"

"Then I'll see you burn for murder!" Kirkpatrick cut in, sternly. "Put that gun away! You're behaving like a cowardly fool!"

For a moment, Toley struggled with a fury that made his eyes pop with the effort at restraint. Finally, he fumbled the gun into his pocket. "All right," he muttered. "I apologize, Wentworth, for the terms I used. But the fact remains that this lawlessness must end! I'll hold… Miss van Sloan until she can prove to me."

WENTWORTH SWUNG away toward his waiting car. Ram Singh stood, rigid as a soldier, to swing open the door and Wentworth flung himself back against the cushions. There was an icy glitter in his blue-gray eyes, and his lips were thin with pressure. He must be careful not to let anger mislead him, but it seemed clear that Toley was motivated by some personal animosity. Did that spring from mere resentment—or was there some other, guilty reason?

Ram Singh was behind the wheel, but Kirkpatrick's car still blocked the way. Impatience goaded Wentworth. He fought to clear his mind of emotional disturbance. Nita, at least, was safe; when he reached the city, he would set his lawyers to work to free her. Nothing more could be done immediately. He tried to concentrate on Wister. The man's strange conduct was explained now; the police would set to work on the kidnapping. Wentworth's own course was plain—the pursuit of the Skull. Perhaps Nita had learned something from the druggist….

Kirkpatrick's car rolled smoothly up the drive and the Daimler followed a moment later. Abruptly, Wentworth jerked forward in the seat. Something like a white mist was rolling up through the moon-shadowed woods ahead; reaching out toward the cars in an ominous cloud!

"Stop! Sound the horn!" Wentworth snapped at Ram Singh. It might be no more than a light fog swept in from the bay, but it was strange that it should spring up now, just before dawn… and curious things had happened this night! Even as Wentworth shouted, as he tugged at the automatic nested beneath his arm, he saw the car ahead swerve violently… and then from the midst of that rolling cloud, machine-guns split the night apart!

Wentworth felt more than heard the shock of bullets against the armor of his car. Men's hoarse cries filled the night, but more startling, even than the attack, were the things he half-glimpsed amid that roiling mist. There were figures that gleamed with a greenish sheen like radium, but they were not the figures of living creatures. The things that Wentworth saw behind the yammering machine-guns were… *the glowing, fleshless skeletons of men!*

CHAPTER 6
THE SKULL SPEAKS

AFTER THAT first shock of vision, Wentworth did not, of course, believe that there were skeletons firing those deadly guns. But, God knows, there was nothing in what he saw to contradict that fact! When the fogs, which he now recognized as a chemical smoke-screen, broke for an instant, he could glimpse those figures whose bones seemed to glow with radium.

"Forward!" he shouted to Ram Singh. "Kirkpatrick's car isn't heavily armored! Cut in front of it. *Hurry!*"

With a snort of power, the Daimler surged forward. Under the skilful guidance of the Sikh, it swerved into the shrubbery and crashed through to slew broadside across the driveway ahead of Kirkpatrick's machine. Revolvers were spitting their meager flame from the police car. Wentworth flung himself to the loop-holes in his own bullet-proof windows and Ram Singh's gun beat out a contrapuntal accompaniment to his own careful shots.

Gun-flame....

Again and again, Wentworth fired at the evanescent figures. His mind was racing with conjecture. Those figures might easily be living men under a grotesque garb... or they might be decoys to turn bullets aside from the real gunners! At the thought, the Spider ceased to throw his lead at those grim outlines, but hunted out the flash of guns as they flickered dimly through the curtain of fog. A yell of pain answered his second shot and, above the smashing of guns, he shouted his discovery.

"The skeletons are decoys!" he cried. "Aim at the gun flashes!"

Even as he spoke, the ambuscade was ended. The enemy guns ceased to flame and there were, suddenly, no more of the mocking silhouettes of fleshless men. For an instant, the aching silence held and then Wentworth saw a fearful thing rushing toward the car from the darkness! It floated smoothly through the air at the height of a man from the ground. A man's head twice normal size—a green-glowing skull in which fiery eyes blazed, to which hone-tight skin still adhered... *and that was all!* A bodiless skull that glided toward him!

"The Skull," Wentworth whispered to himself, even while he laid his careful aim upon the apparition. *"The Skull...."*

His gun crashed and there, in the forehead of that ghastly glaring thing, a black bullet-hole appeared! Still the head floated on! The gruesome jaws worked and there echoed across the scene a rasping and mocking laughter!

"Shoot, fools!" the Skull cried. "Shoot... and learn how futile are bullets against the Skull! You are doomed. Your city is doomed! *Flee while there yet is time!"*

Wentworth's bullets were tearing through and through that fearsome skull, pocking it with lead-ripped holes. Once more the jarring laughter sounded and then... *the Skull vanished!* It was as abrupt as that. One instant, the ominous head was gliding toward him through the night and the next instant, it was gone! There was nothing at all there in the blackness of the overgrown woods except the last remnants of the smoke-screen vanishing among the trees.

In an instant, Wentworth flung from the protection of his car and, with freshly loaded guns, charged into the darkness.

"Lights, Ram Singh!" he shouted as he ran. "Throw lights here!"

An instant later, the auxiliary spotlight of the Daimler splashed across the underbrush. It danced over the black boles of trees, gleamed on the last remnants of the chemical mist— and found nothing else. The woods were empty, deserted. They might have been firing at so many ghosts... Wentworth swore under his breath as he raced for the gates that gave onto the street; plunged out into the roadway with his guns ready in his fist. Nothing here; absolutely nothing....

Lights were springing up in the houses scattered among their wide-spread grounds. He could hear a man calling excitedly from Wister's house. Cautiously, Wentworth spilled light from a small pocket-flash on the gravel of the street, but he could find no trace of a fugitive gunman. He whirled and ran back toward his car. In the dazzle of the spotlight, he could now see the jagged, white tears that bullets had ripped in the bark of trees, but there was not even a remnant of one of those glowing skeletons, or of the talking Skull. The whole thing was mad as a nightmare; ridiculous... and strangely terrifying.

WENTWORTH DARTED toward Kirkpatrick's car, heard the commissioner's voice snapping orders over the two-way radio of the machine. He whipped open the door. "No trace of their car," Wentworth said, "but the surface of the street is pretty hard. That Skull trick delayed us while they were all getting away."

Kirkpatrick's face was taut with anger. There was blood on his temple and the side windows of the car were in fragments; the bullet-proof windshield frosted over. The driver was a motionless huddle.

"They got Morgan, damn them," Kirkpatrick said hoarsely. "Toley took one through the left wrist. Thanks for pushing your car in ahead of us, Dick. Otherwise..." He closed his lips rigidly, as the radio signal of the police announcer hummed in the receiver.

"Calling Car O-one-thirteen," the man said rapidly. "Come in!"

That was the call for Kirkpatrick's car and Kirkpatrick answered steadily, "Car O-one-thirteen reporting. Now in Bayside. Come in."

The announcer's voice was vibrant with excitement. "Been trying to raise you since three o'clock, O-one-thirteen. Your radio must have been out of commission. The Spider with a gang of other men attacked the officers arresting Van Sloan at Thirty-Third and Park. Three officers were killed and two wounded. Van Sloan was carried off. Routine pursuit. Any special orders? Come in, O-one-thirteen."

Wentworth's hand trembled visibly on the door. It was not the mention of the Spider, though he realized with a quick clarity that at the hour mentioned, he had indeed been in the Spider's garb... He had no alibi. But Nita... He knew without the slightest question that it was the Skull who had done this, not only kidnapping Nita, but striking a shrewd blow at the Spider's reputation. Nita... in the power of the Skull!

He said hoarsely, "Back to New York, Kirk. If that fiend has harmed Nita..." He swung away from the car.

"Just a minute, Dick," Kirkpatrick said sharply, then spoke into the radio. "General alarm for Nita van Sloan and the Spider. Remember, the Spider is armed and dangerous. Take no chances. Announce to the papers under my name that the Spider apparently has stepped over the line at last and thrown in with criminals... with the criminals who are spreading poison through the city! It is war to the finish! That is all!"

71

His eyes burned into Wentworth's. "I have been afraid for a long time that the Spider would step over the line some day," he said steadily. "I believe I have said as much to you, Dick. A man cannot make himself prosecutor, judge and executioner... He cannot take the law into his own hands time and again without someday beginning to feel that he is above the law. But no man is, Dick. Not even the Spider! And when he kills some of my own men...."

Toley's voice was strained with pain as he clutched his wounded wrist. "Why talk in riddles, Kirkpatrick?" he said thickly. "It's plain, isn't it? Why should the Spider kidnap Nita van Sloan, unless the Spider is also—*Richard Wentworth!* Where were you at three o'clock, Wentworth?"

Wentworth could see the inflexible purpose in Kirkpatrick's set and bloodstained face. He himself was shaken with fear for Nita; with the nightmare horror of the recent ambuscade. He ignored Toley.

"Wait now, Kirk," he said. "Wait a minute..." He drew in a deep breath, fought for clarity of thought. "I didn't even know Nita had been arrested until you told me there in Wister's place. You must know that. In God's name, why should I—assuming that I was the Spider—have to murder policemen to get Nita free from a ridiculous charge which even you did not believe? Is this the first time that a criminal has masqueraded in the Spider's costume? Is the Spider the only one who would have reason to kidnap Nita? What about these devils that jumped us here tonight—the Skull!"

Kirkpatrick's face did not change, "Where were you at three o'clock, Dick?" he demanded.

Wentworth shrugged, "I left home a few minutes before three o'clock to come out here. On the way, I ran into some poisoning cases; a woman with a child. I took her to the hospital." Wentworth cut off his words abruptly. In his excitement, he had committed a fatal blunder. It was true that he had rescued the woman's child—but he had worn the garb of the Spider!

Kirkpatrick relaxed a bit." That should be easy to verify," he said. "What hospital? Did you get the woman's name?"

Wentworth feigned an outburst of temper. "No, and I didn't take her fingerprints! Maybe she was the Spider! Listen, I'm going back to New York. While we stand here talking, Nita... God knows what is happening to her! If you want me, send your men to arrest me!"

He stormed back to his car, ignored the sharp accents of Kirkpatrick's voice calling to him. He was frantic with the need for haste, and he would not be arrested now... not if it meant fighting his way clear! He flung himself into the car and his signal to Ram Singh sent the Daimler surging forward. It tore a wide half-circle through the shrubs, rocked back into the driveway and boomed through the gate-way, into the street. The motor's note became deep and powerful.

AGAINST THE cushions, Wentworth forced relaxation upon his taut-nerved body. It was possible that, over the repaired radio, Kirkpatrick had put out a call for his arrest, but Wentworth doubted it. That was an arrest Kirkpatrick would compel himself to make in person, if necessity ever arose. Toley would goad him with doubts….

Wentworth lifted slow hands and covered his face. There was no question as to the reason for Nita's kidnapping. The Skull wanted the leverage of a hostage against him… and that was a thing Wentworth could not permit. If he could not find and free Nita at once, the Spider could make only one answer to the Skull's ultimatum. The Spider would not, could not turn aside from the path of service—not even for Nita's sweet sake!

Wentworth pulled his hands down rigidly, took out his guns and methodically cleaned and checked them. There was utterly no expression in his face unless the rigid set of his jaw could be called that. He forced himself to consider his course of action.

If he could only arrive at the reason behind these senseless murders, he would know then where to hunt for the Skull. Aside from that, his only chance was to form direct contact with the killer himself. Nothing more could be learned from Wister, over whose home police guard was established now. Over seeming aeons of time, he recalled his temporary suspicions of Beck. That source of inquiry was still open, of course. But at best, his role must be a minor one, and remote from the Skull himself. Wentworth remembered that he had pledged himself to hunt down the Spider… He fell limply back against the seat and laughter that was close to hysteria pushed at his constrained throat.

Afterward, he was calmer. There was another trail, of course— the trail that the false Spider had left from the scene of his attack upon the police captors of Nita. He caught up the speaking-tube.

"Thirty-third and Park, Ram Singh," he ordered crisply.

From Triborough Bridge, he turned his heavy eyes toward the skyline of Manhattan, its spires rising in graceful silhouette against the reddening dawn sky. There was majesty there that caught at the throat like grief… and deathly horror stalked its streets. How much of horror Wentworth was to learn too soon….

It came while the Daimler was boring its way swiftly down Park Avenue toward Grand Central and the ramps that wove around it to bridge Forty-second Street. Unconsciously, his eyes sought the clock between the twin arched entrance ways of the ramps, and a choked curse burned on his lips. Something was dangling from that clock—something that glowed with a faint greenish light there in the dusk against the building!

Wentworth found himself straining forward tautly in his seat, his guns locked in white-knuckled fists. Swiftly, his eyes probed the entrances of the ramps, searched the street. It was deserted, and nowhere was there any hint of attack. Wentworth shot a single swift glance behind him and caught a glimpse of a car. That would be Kirkpatrick. His gaze swung back to that dangling something, and a tortured breath caught in his lungs. It was a human skeleton that swung from the clock—a human skeleton with a woman's dark, long hair blowing gently in the dawn breeze!

Wentworth beat his knotted fists upon his knees. When his voice came out, it was harsh, unrecognizable. "Stop by the clock, Ram Singh!"

He could see more now. He could see that, though every

shred of flesh had been stripped from the body of that skeleton, the head itself was intact… the face beneath that frame of
dark, lovely hair was unharmed. God, in heaven, what cruelty!
What fiendish madman had devised this thing! He still could
not identify the face. It was too far away, too dark. *God, this thing
could not be….*

From the driver's seat, the harsh outlandish curses of Ram
Singh thudded against Wentworth's ears. He heard the melo-
dious blast of Kirkpatrick's horn, then the brief muted wail of
his siren. His senses recorded those things; his mind did not. All
his being was centered on the desperate, shrinking endeavor to
read that hidden face. Abruptly, a blade of light flicked out and
touched the grisly thing. Ram Singh had brought the spotlight
deliberately into play. For an instant, it glanced across the stark
white bones and tossed a grotesque shadow, huge as death and
as menacing, across the front of the building. Then it centered
on the face.

A great cry tore Wentworth's throat There was a shaking that
wrenched at his whole body… but he had been spared the ulti-
mate horror. It was not Nita's body that dangled from the clock.
It was that of a sweet-faced girl whose portrait Wentworth had
seen no more than an hour before. The kidnapers had fulfilled
their pledge and Nona Malvern, the ward of Samuel Wister,
had died… *terribly!*

Wentworth flung from his car as it jerked to a halt and his
wincing eyes turned upward to the poor thing on the clock. It
would be horrible enough merely to find Nona Malvern dead
there, but to see that stripped skeleton with the head grotesquely

intact… Wentworth shuddered and turned away, staggering. It was when he turned that he saw the message that was scrawled in letters of scarlet across the face of the building:

> Fools' skeletons and their faces
> Will be found in public place.
> Unless they obey.…

And appended to that crude jingle, doubly ghastly in its joking treatment of this horror, was the signature. The grinning, mocking portrait of a skull!

And Nita was in that fiend's power!

CHAPTER 7
DEATH MARCHES ON

IT WAS broad daylight when Richard Wentworth, drunk with fatigue and horror, made his way home at last. All trails had pinched out. There was nothing to indicate when, within hours, Nona Malvern's skeleton had been hung on the clock, nor any trace of the men who had done it. They had chosen their time well… before dawn, on a spring Sunday and there had been almost no traffic; hence no witnesses. At the scene of Nita's kidnapping, there had been no evidence except that Wentworth had found Nita's handkerchief, and on it there were a number of red dots made with a lipstick in an eccentric pattern.

Wentworth studied the thing as Ram Singh rolled the car finally toward the house through the Sabbath-quiet of the streets, but his eyes were blurred and his mind seemed filled with lead. He tried to use the dots as the points of letters, and couldn't. They were just dots; straggling irregularly across the linen:

    •   •   •   •   •

    •   •   •   •   •

    • •   •   •

      •   •

             •

             •

By his private elevator, Wentworth ascended directly to his suite and there flung himself down for the two hours sleep he had allowed himself. He could not afford the time—but he must rest. His acute mind, his lightning-swift reflexes were slowed. In this condition, it would do him no good to track down the Skull; he would fall easy prey to the simplest trap... With the concentration that marked everything he attempted, Wentworth plunged himself into a blankness of spirit and mind that brought sleep almost instantly.

Promptly at the end of the time he had allowed himself, Wentworth woke of his own accord and snapped himself back to normal with a swift violent round of calisthenics and a plunge into the icy waters of his pool. When he emerged, his lithe, tanned body—marked by the scars that were the Spider's only medals for valor—was taut and alert again. His mind was racing. Before he could signal for Jenkyns, the old butler entered his room with a perfectly appointed breakfast table. Jenkyns' wrinkled, ruddy face was creased in a smile.

"Jackson is home from the hospital, sir," he reported, "and

there is a gentleman waiting to see you. His card is beside your plate, Master Richard."

Wentworth nodded while he caught up the newspaper. "Miss Moulin?" he said. "Mr. Beck?"

"Waiting for word from you, sir," Jenkyns reported. "Mr. Beck refused to let Miss Moulin leave except on specific orders from you."

Wentworth's eyes were combing the front page, of the Sunday paper. Even the pontifical *Times* was hysterical with eight-column headlines. A hundred and three persons had been stricken with poisoned medicines overnight. Of those, eighty-five had died! Every drugstore in town had been ordered closed pending a close check on their stock. Three other wholesale distributors besides Wister's Eastern Drug Company were involved. Against that mounting toll of horror, the kidnapping of Nita and the murder of the three policemen seemed unimportant. The Wister kidnapping with its macabre, pitiful ending had come too late to receive adequate display.

Wentworth flung the paper from him and his eyes held a fierce fire as he forced himself to eat the breakfast Jenkyns had prepared. He must get back into the battle. There was a possible lead in the druggists whose stores had been the distribution points of poison. The murder of the man who had escaped with Nita the night before indicated that he might have told something, had he lived, and... Wentworth's eyes fell on the card beside his plate—the card of the man who was waiting to see him—and a startled oath rose to his lips. Then he smiled grimly.

"You may tell Mr. Samuel Wister," he said quietly, "that I'll be with him in five minutes, Jenkyns!"

IT WAS actually four minutes later that fully dressed, his eyes as keen as though rested by a full night's sleep, Wentworth strode into the drawing-room and bowed to the broad, dynamic figure which stood beside the open terrace doors.

"Sorry to have kept you waiting, Mr. Wister," he said pleasantly. "Believe me, you have my deepest sympathy."

Wister turned and there was a heaviness in all his movements. The shadows under his pale eyes were liverish, made his whole face haggard. "I come to you," he said, "because you have Kirkpatrick's ear; because I do not dare—after what has happened—to go to the police directly. There are things the police should know."

Wentworth nodded, his eyes keen on the man's face. At his

invitation Wister sank into a chair, closed his eyes. "I blame myself for a great deal of what has happened," he said, without expression. "This man who calls himself the Skull phoned me a week ago and demanded that the Eastern Drug Company join a protective association with dues of ten thousand dollars a week! I thought he was a crank, and... ignored it."

Wentworth's face was impassive, but his mind leaped on ahead of Wister's speech. So that was the motive behind these poisonings, the old protection racket in a new and ghastly form! The Skull's methods were utterly inhuman—but Wentworth well knew they would prove effective! After even this one night's horrors, there was not a druggist or wholesaler in town who would dare to refuse payments!

"I shall pay, of course, now," Wister's words echoed Wentworth's thoughts. "Out of humanity, I can do nothing else. My men have been working all night to discover how the poison was planted in our medicines. We have no slightest clue. The goods in our store rooms seem to be all right."

Wentworth shook his head. There was something wrong with this set-up. No racketeer could hope to escape prosecution, no matter what repressive horrors he practiced... Wentworth remembered the pitiful skeleton of Nona Malvern and suddenly he was not sure. What man would testify in the face of that threat? Slowly, a cold smile crept across his lips. Well, there was a solution that would require no man's testimony in court... *the way of the Spider!* Yes, the racketeer had feared that. He had his hostage against such extra-legal action. He had... *Nita.*

The pallor of Wentworth's face matched that of Samuel

Wister, but he spoke steadily. "Tell me the name of this protective association and the rest of it."

Wister rolled his head heavily against the back of the chair. "I don't know," he said thickly. "I can only hope that the Skull will give me another chance. I'm waiting for him to call, and when he does, I'll pay! As you have guessed, there was no demand of ransom for... for Nona. She was simply hostage that I would not notify the police. My wife... I put her on a ship for France this morning. Anything I can do I will willingly undertake. Just tell me."

Wentworth promised grimly and it was with impatience that he saw his guest to the door.

As soon as Wister was gone, Wentworth dashed to his rooms, caught up the handkerchief that he had found on the scene of Nita's kidnapping. The druggist, he was remembering now, had been making a phone call when he fell dead of poison. It was logical, wasn't it, that after his fright he would be attempting to communicate his surrender to the Skull? And Nita knew the trick that Wentworth had on occasion used... of picking up the static electrical impulse of each click of a dial phone in a radio receiver! Those clicks would come too rapidly to be counted mentally, but it was possible to record them, a tap of the finger for each click, *a lipstick dot on a handkerchief for each click!*

Wentworth stared at the dots again, counted them swiftly. They gave the number 34236, or conversely 63243. Wentworth shook his head. The number was two digits less than was used on New York dial telephones—but he was sure he was right.

Probably, the radio had not warmed up in time for Nita to catch the first two.

Wentworth jabbed a signal button while he checked his theory. The only question was… What number had the druggist been calling? It might be as innocent as his own home… There was a light tap at his door and Jackson stepped into the room, a neat gauze bandage about his head. His strong, muscular face was pale.

Wentworth smiled, "Not too badly hurt for work, Jackson?" he asked.

"Try me, sir," Jackson said curtly. "I'm just aching to get my hands on those mugs!"

Wentworth held out the handkerchief and explained his theory. "You can eliminate at once all exchanges whose final digit is neither three nor six," he said. "The telephone company will help, I won't have time to see either Beck or Miss Moulin this morning. Miss Moulin is to remain here for safety. Beck will await my orders by telephone. I'll call back for the information on that phone number."

While Wentworth was speaking, he had discarded his coat and was strapping on the twin holsters that carried his automatics beneath his arms. The grimness of his jaw increased. "It's possible that a gentleman who calls himself the Skull will telephone to make threats. You will know what to do. He has Miss Nita a prisoner!"

Jackson swore harshly. "I'll know what to do!" he cried. "But, sir… you're not going out alone?"

Wentworth was punching into his coat again. He briefly

touched the automatics beneath his arms. "Not entirely alone, Jackson!" he said softly.

THE ELEVATOR dropped him swiftly to the underground corridor that connected with the garage. Not for him this time the conspicuous black length of the Daimler. He chose a somewhat battered coupé whose worn paint-job was belied by the sweet, powerful precision of the motor. Wentworth sent the car swiftly through the streets. He had communicated to Kirkpatrick the information given him by Wister and the police would make arrangements to trap the Skull should he call again. Wentworth hoped that he himself had a more direct and swift contact!

The Skull might well play a cautious game with a man like Wister, but with the lesser prey, the owners of pharmacies, he must have arranged a simpler method of pay-off. Wentworth did not expect, in questioning the druggists whose supplies had been poisoned, to learn anything that would take him straight to the Skull. But he hoped to connect with an underling, and after that... after that, nothing, not even the imminent danger to Nita, could swerve the Spider from the stern trail of justice!

But he must move swiftly. Men were working night and day in an effort to speed the check of medical supplies, but the very fact that wholesale stocks were uncontaminated showed how cleverly the Skull was working. Even if entire stores full of supplies were declared harmless, the reopening of the pharmacies might well signal a new series of poisonings! Meantime, the thousands of sick persons in the city were without medicines when they must have to survive. To the scores of poison dead, there might well be added hundreds, thousands more of these victims!

The first two druggists whom Wentworth sought were, he was told at their homes, undergoing questioning at the hands of the police. At the third place, Wentworth found a man who had just limply returned from the precinct station. Terror turned the man's face gray at Wentworth's first question.

"I have a wife and child!" he cried hoarsely. "Do you think we don't know what happened to Nona Malvern and why? My wife, my child… and you want me to talk?"

Wentworth's smile was grave as he looked from the man to his wife, who stood at his elbow, twisting thin hands together helplessly. "Oh, why can't they leave us alone?" she cried. "We have done nothing. We only want to live in peace."

"Yes," Wentworth's voice was curiously gentle. "Yes, you want to live… in peace." It was for the sake of people like these that he had always been willing to plunge himself into conflict with the underworld; for their welfare, he and Nita had foregone the happiness they could have found together—because of them, Nita was now a prisoner of the Skull!

"I can't blame you for your fright," he went on. "I'm Richard Wentworth. If you read the papers this morning you know that the woman I love is in the hands of the same man who…" Stiffness crept across Wentworth's face, made his smile twisted. "The same man who did—what was done to Nona Malvern! I won't do anything so futile as promise to protect you. But I would give a great deal for one little piece of information. With that money, you could leave the city. You could, perhaps, go abroad and start over again."

The woman's hand worked on her husband's shoulder. Hoarsely, the man said, "You know what you're asking?"

"Perfectly," Wentworth nodded. "If you refuse me, I cannot blame you... but until the murderer is caught, this slaughter will go on! If you begin paying racket money, that will not be the end! I want only one little bit of information: How were you supposed to pay this money?"

The druggist was young. His high forehead was pale under the black sweep of his hair. His dark eyes showed suffering. "God help me," he whispered. "God help me... I'll tell you, but I want no pay! These murderers... Listen, I don't know how I was supposed to pay. There was a protective association, and I have its phone number...."

He began to fumble in his pockets—and, from the hall behind him, Wentworth caught the rasp of a footstep! It had a furtive sound, as if the person there sought to conceal his presence! Wentworth did not wait to throw a glance in that direction. He went toward the druggist in a hard, low dive, hurled him and his wife backward across the room. In the same instant, a gun blasted out behind him. Wentworth heard the woman utter a strangled, high cry, saw her scrambling across the floor toward the room beyond.

The druggist lay where he had fallen, but whether he had been killed by the bullet or stunned by the fall, there was no chance to learn. Wentworth turned as he fell and his shoulders struck the floor in the same moment that his twin, heavy automatics thudded against his palms.

THE GUNMAN was crouched on the stairs, hidden behind palings and newel post so that only the glint of his gun-muzzle and a fraction of his head showed. Impossible for Wentworth to hit that target. But both automatics thundered in his hands. Splinters flew from the palings. The din of the guns was terrific in the narrow hall. Wentworth hit the floor and steadied himself, punched a bullet through the newel post behind which the man crouched. There was a sharp, muffled cry, then footsteps clattered down the steps.

In a long leap, Wentworth reached the railing, leaned over. He saw the man's white face twisted about to stare up him fearfully as he ran, saw the spurt of flame from a hurriedly fired gun. Wentworth was not hurried. His left-hand automatic dropped into line on the man's left shoulder and he squeezed the trigger. Then a shout of chagrin leaped to his lips and he tried to stay the shot, to turn it aside… too late.

Even as he touched the trigger, the fugitive gunman ducked his head… to the left! The bullet, striking the back of his skull, picked his feet up off the steps and hurled him in a macabre somersault. He struck the wall and lay unmoving, a broken travesty of what had been a man. Afterward, there was silence for seconds, and then, somewhere, a woman started screaming.

Wentworth went toward the druggist's apartment with long, quick strides. In the doorway, he stopped and his face twisted bitterly. He knew now that his leap had been too late; that the first bullet had sped true. Its bloody trace was there in the middle of that boy's splendid forehead. His wife… Wentworth was abruptly aware of the aching silence of the apartment! With a curse, he bounded across the room, into the one beyond. A window was open there and the black, iron straps of a fire-escape were just beyond. A child's bed was empty.

Wentworth flung himself at the window. Had the woman fled in terror with her child… or had worse happened? Had the men of the Skull attacked from both sides at once? He peered out into the back court of the apartment building, down between the wash-hung clothes lines. He saw nothing, no sign of the woman or her child; no disturbance. There was more noise now in the building, doors slamming and shouted inquiries.

Damn it, he was responsible for this thing! If he had not come asking questions… This could mean only that the men of the Skull had been following him! He shook his head. That was wrong. He could not have been trailed without his knowledge, even if the Skull followed so mild a course! Bullets from ambush would have been his portion. It meant, instead, that they were watching these druggists like hawks….

Wentworth spun away from the window. The druggist apparently had the phone number written down. If the Spider had been the cause of his death, the least the Spider could do would be to avenge him! Only it must be quick, before the police came. In the doorway, Wentworth stopped dead in his tracks. His eyes swept the room and then, with an oath, he was bounding toward the hallway again! Where the druggist had lain, there was a little red smear… nothing else. The man himself had vanished!

Gun knotted in his fist, Wentworth raced down the stairs. He paused for an instant beside the man he had slain and searched him for some clue that might point the way to the Skull's hideout. Save for the usual skeleton talisman, his body gave no helpful evidence.

For a long moment, Wentworth stared down at the man. He made it a rule never to use the seal of the Spider while in his own identity, but here it was more than justified. He must answer these repeated attempts to link him with the work of the poisoners, put the terror of retribution upon the Skull's men! He laid the grotesque small skeleton on the man's chest and, on his forehead, he ground in the violent red seal of the Spider!

From the head of the stairs, a man's voice spoke harshly, "Drop that gun, Spider, or I'll pump you full of lead!"

CHAPTER 8
A CLUE AT LAST

WENTWORTH DID not wait for the man above to voice his threat. The instant he spoke, Wentworth hurled himself aside in the dimness of the hallway. The walls rocked with the blast of a shotgun and some of the pellets plucked at Wentworth's coat! His gun swiveled upward... and just in time he checked himself. It was a man in police uniform up there with a riot-gun! The man was plunging down the steps, the gun clutched ready in his hands. There wasn't a chance in the world of Wentworth's making the next flight of steps downward before that murderous weapon blasted at him again!

Still reeling from his first dodging leap, Wentworth threw

himself at a near-by door. The flimsy portal crashed open and Wentworth pitched through, head down, doubling frantically into an acrobat's fall that would bring him up on his feet running. Once more, that terrific concussion hammered through the hall. The air ripped apart within inches of Wentworth's face; his hat was blasted from his head.

Swift as light, Wentworth's eyes flicked over the room into which he had plunged. It was empty… and its only opening was an overhead skylight! He was trapped—and out there in the hallway he had used the Spider's seal! Trapped, and he dared not even allow the policeman to see his face!

It would be impossible to get out through the sky-light, even if he could reach it before the policeman drew an inescapable bead on him with the riot-gun. True, a heavy pole used to open the skylight, dangled from the catch. Wentworth's eyes narrowed in swift planning. His one hope… He seized the pole and started to climb up it with the frantic, exaggerated movements of fright. The pole swung erratically… and the man burst in through the doorway.

"Don't shoot!" Wentworth screamed. "Don't shoot! I'll surrender! For God's sake, don't shoot again! You got me…."

The man crouched a half dozen feet away by the door, the shotgun ready across his chest. As the pole swung wildly back and forth, Wentworth could glimpse him out of the corner of his eye, but he carefully kept his face turned away.

"Come down out of that," the man ordered. "There are three more shells in this gun and I'd like the chance to blow you to bits! You damned cop-killing crook!"

"Sure," Wentworth babbled. "Sure, I'll come down! Just don't shoot!"

He let go and dropped, sprawling toward the floor, landed on all fours within a yard of the cop… and in the same instant, he struck. He used his hands as a pivot and lashed outward with both feet at once! One foot slammed aside the barrel of that murderous gun; the other drove with neat precision against the man's jaw. Once more, that gun spewed out its butcher's load of death! The concussion seemed to crush in Wentworth's eardrums, but he reeled dizzily to his feet. The man was out cold on the floor… and the charge had missed.

Wentworth stooped over the man. His kick had been well guided. He was unconscious, would be out for possibly ten or fifteen minutes, but no serious harm had been inflicted. Without hesitation, Wentworth caught up his hat and then heaved the body to his shoulders; ran along the hall toward the stairs. If this man had come by way of the roof—and there was no other way in which he could have taken Wentworth from behind—it meant that there was a heavy force of men below! The building must be surrounded!

Wentworth raced down two floors, then he yanked out his gun and fired two shots in the ceiling. He backed down the last flight of stairs with the uniformed body across his shoulders and while he went down, the gun racketed in his fist.

"They're trapped," he yelled. "They're trapped up there!"

He heard excited shouts behind him, but did not turn his head. He fired a last burst of shots up the steps, turned and with his head low, leaped reeling down the last of the stairway.

He glimpsed three men in the lower hall, another just barging in through the front door. How many more were out there he could not guess, but he knew that he had walked into a carefully prepared trap. How the criminals had managed to snatch away the druggist's body without running into the police themselves he could not understand, but… A shock ran along Wentworth's nerves. Not five feet away from him was a man in the blue police uniform. There was nothing wrong with the uniform… *but the man wore tan shoes!*

That single glimpse was enough. Wentworth knew in that flashing instant that these were not genuine police officers, but criminals in disguise! Police regulations required black shoes and no man would be allowed to go out on duty in shoes of any other color. In the same instant Wentworth was in action. A quick heave of his shoulders hurled the unconscious man he carried against the three who were grouped together at the foot of the steps!

As they went down, Wentworth sprang straight at the fourth man in the doorway. His gun was swinging up. Wentworth's automatic was ready in his fist… but he did not fire. There was just the faint chance that this might be a genuine police officer, a late arrival… Wentworth threw his automatic and his aim was true. It caught the man's gun-wrist just as he was squeezing the trigger. Lead tore past Wentworth's side as he leaped and his fist finished the swift job.

THE HIGH shriek of police sirens filled the air. There was no chance to get to his car, parked a half block away, and take flight. Wentworth dodged into the basement entrance of the building next door, bounded through the musty cellar. Seconds later, he drew himself out of a narrow window into the back court and vaulted a fence.

Presently, in an adjoining street, he was circling back toward the scene of the attack!

His gray-blue eyes, secretive under lowered lids, were dark with fury. Every move he had made in this battle with the Skull had been hounded by disaster... and always it was the innocent that suffered. He knew without question that it would be futile for him to try farther to get information from the druggists. Terrorism would shut their mouths. Another thought forced its way into his brain. If he had been recognized by the criminals—if the truth got back to the Skull—Nita would pay the penalty! He must work fast, fast....

Wentworth checked at the corner of the street into which police cars were jammed now. It was dangerous to go back there. If anyone had seen his flight, they would be able to identify him at least by his clothing. And there were rents in it where the shotgun slugs had just missed his body! No matter. He had to get close. If those criminals escaped....

There were men in police blue about the entrance of the build-

NITA VAN SLOAN

ing and scores of people from adjoining houses were crowding out into the street. Some, at least, of those men at the door were the real police. Surely, the criminals could not be mingling with them! Their deception could not be carried so far. Wentworth pushed on into the street, mixed with the Sunday crowd. His eyes keenly studied the faces of the officers. The criminals were not among them.

Sharp doubt stabbed Wentworth. Had they made their escape while he circled to evade pursuit? Even while the question sprang up in his mind, one of the police came out of the building with a discarded uniform coat in his hands... and Wentworth knew! Even this chance had failed him!

Now what?

There remained then only the slender clue of the telephone number Nita had recorded on her handkerchief... and that might have been an entirely innocent call! Wentworth swung on his heel and entered a corner lunch room and made the call to his home. Jackson answered promptly... No, there had been no phoned threats from the Skull. There had been nothing at all. But Jackson had a long list of numbers, any one of which might be the one Nita had partly recorded—twenty-five, in fact.

Wentworth swore under his breath. There was so little time, and all those numbers would have to be checked carefully lest the criminals take alarm at any one of his inquiries.

"Isn't there anything suspicious about any one of them?" he asked quietly. "Is any of them the number of a drug concern, or...."

"There is one curious thing, sir," Jackson's voice lowered. "One of the numbers on this list is the phone of this young detective here in the house, Donald Beck! His office is in the Remarque Building."

For an instant, Wentworth stared incredulously at the phone over which this message had come. Beck... the Skull's hireling?

He shook his head. It was possible, of course. It was also possible that the dead druggist had simply been calling on him for help....

"Nothing else?" he asked slowly.

"Not another thing, sir," Jackson said. "Most of them are private phones."

Wentworth said steadily, "See that Beck stays there, for a half hour then have Ram Singh take him to his office. I'll be there! Find out all you can about those other phones and their subscribers without alarming anyone. And, Jackson, keep a careful watch over the place! The Skull's men are masquerading as police now!"

SWINGING FROM the booth, Wentworth caught a taxi and sped toward the Remarque Building while his mind speculated on the possible guilt of Donald Beck. There had been suspicious circumstances about Beck before this, but the man himself seemed so frank and open....

It took twenty minutes to reach the Remarque Building and in that time the taxi radio brayed out endless alarms. The news-casters were pumping out excited words about the poisonings, swelling the terrorism by which the Skull hoped to rule. Already, they had got hold of the fact that the druggist whom Wentworth questioned had been attacked. They said the man, his wife and child had all vanished.

Horror gripped Wentworth at the thought. Good Lord, had that poor woman also been seized by the Skull? He had been sure she had merely fled to safety with her child. The memory of the pitiful remains of Nona Malvern burned like fire in his brain. He beat his fists softly on his knees with the driving need for speed. If he could track down the Skull quickly enough....

The Remarque Building was a down-at-the-heel office structure on a side street off Times Square. The elevator, when Wentworth had rung up the watchman, creaked and swayed as it labored upward. As soon as the gate had closed, Wentworth stalked on silent feet toward the door on which was painted:

DONALD BECK
INVESTIGATIONS

Wentworth's eyes swept the hallway, but found no indications of a watch kept here. The door resisted his hand and he slid out a slim hooked tool of surgical steel, a lock-pick. Moments later, the bolt yielded to shrewd manipulation and Wentworth pushed the door carefully open. Something scraped softly along the floor and, inside, Wentworth stared down in amazement at the waste-basket which caught mail dropped through the slot in the door. The basket was full and overflowing. Half the floor of the room was covered with letters!

Swiftly, Wentworth caught up a handful of the letters. Each one was thick and stiff with the crackle of the paper inside... and five of those in his hand were addressed from various drug stores! Wentworth ripped open the envelopes and he stared down at sheaf after sheaf of currency! There were no letters, no messages, save in each envelope was a little slip with the name of a drugstore and the amount of money noted below it! Wentworth's hand knotted into a white fist about the money. Well, there was no longer any doubt, was there? This was the protection money the Skull had demanded of the drug stores, and this was the pay-off station… *the office of Donald Beck!*

With long, silent strides, Wentworth crossed to the inner office of the detective and there was a knife-gash of a frown between his brows. He was remembering his earlier deductions. He had hoped through Nita's clue to find some minor member of the gang, for surely the Skull would not allow in general circulation a number which would lead directly to him! That would explain matters, of course. Donald Beck was merely a small link in the chain that would lead to the Skull, perhaps the weakest link… Wentworth's lips moved in a grim smile at the thought. It was a link that was soon broken!

With swift efficiency, Wentworth began to ransack the office. It was habit, engendered of long nights of secret work, that made him work silently. It was experience that presently revealed, fastened beneath the desk, the ear of a dictograph! An oath sprang to Wentworth's lips… and died there, unuttered, as the significance of that listening device struck him. Either the police were suspicious of Beck and had set up a plant here… or the criminals were keeping him under surveillance! That might mean the criminals doubted his loyalty to the Skull, or it might mean that Beck was innocent!

Even while those thoughts were racing through Wentworth's mind, he was in action. He did not disturb the dictograph, but his sensitive fingers traced its tiny wires under the rug to a far corner of the room where they passed through the floor! In a single long stride, Wentworth reached the window of Beck's office and eased it open soundlessly. There was a window directly below. It was partly open and the shade was drawn down tightly! It was a matter of moments to reach the hall and descended the fire-stair of this deserted building to the floor below. The door of the office beneath Beck's bore no sign. Were the men inside police—or criminals? Wentworth's lips moved in a slight, cold smile. He'd soon find out!

He had brought with him the emptied waste-basket from Beck's office, together with scraps of paper and a tattered shirt found in the desk drawer. On the metal bottom of the basket, he soon had a small fire going. He thrust it close against the door and watched the draft of that open window begin to suck the odorous smoke of the burning rag in through the crack around the door. Then he flattened against the wall to wait. Luckily, since it was Sunday, there was small chance that anyone else would be disturbed.

Now....

Tensely, Wentworth listened for the first indication that the smoke of the fire had been noticed. He held no gun in his hand, but there was an alert and eager light in his eyes. Police or criminal, his course must be the same. If it were the law, he must make amends as best he could... His acutely attuned ears caught an exclamation from inside the office and, with gloved hand, he caught up the fire basket in which only the smoldering rag remained. Footsteps beat hurriedly across the room, the door was suddenly whipped open....

INSTANTLY, WENTWORTH was in action. He flipped the smoldering contents of the basket in through the doorway straight at the still invisible man and... charged after it. A man was reeling backward across the room, arm thrown protectively across his face. He clenched a gun in his fist! He glimpsed Wentworth and jerked up the gun....

Wentworth's fists swung in perfect rhythm. The left batted down the muzzle of the revolver. His right lanced under that up-lifted arm and clicked home to the jaw! In a single long bound, Wentworth went past him toward the door of the inner office... It was empty!

Wentworth pivoted and, with quick efficiency, yanked the semi-conscious man up from the floor and bound him with his own torn clothing to a chair. Since the man worked here alone, there could no longer be any doubt. Police always worked a plant in pairs... A swift search confirmed his guess. Within moments and Wentworth held on his palm the tiny wooden figure of a skeleton! That symbol of the Skull had seemed grotesque and childish when first Wentworth's eyes had fallen on it, but now it had taken on a devilish meaning. In that bit of wood and twisted wire was an echo of the horror he had seen the night before... of Nona Malvern's poor body, and the promise of horror to come which it signified!

Wentworth turned to the reviving man and there was a cold fire in his eyes which wiped the sneer off the criminal's face. Wentworth did not speak to him. Instead, he recovered his wastebasket and into it piled scraps of paper that were scattered over the floor of the room. He snaked out a drawer of the desk and with powerful hands snapped the partitions into firewood. When he had the basket fixed to his satisfaction, he crossed to his prisoner and began to bind it in the man's lap.

THE SPIDER

Wentworth fought with a sense of utter
unreality and unreasoning dread!

"Hey!" the man said hoarsely. "Hey, wait a minute… God, you ain't going to do a thing like that!… For God's sake, mister.…"

Wentworth's smile was wintry and thin. He struck a match.

"For God's sake, mister, give me a chance!"

With a steady hand, Wentworth touched fire to a scrap of paper on the opposite side of the basket from the man's body, near the top. It would burn very slowly from there… The man broke into incoherent pleading, his eyes strained wide as they stared down at the slowly spreading fire.

"I know you boys who work for the Skull," Wentworth said, his voice incongruously gentle. "I know you're tough, so it's a good idea to soften you up right away, before I ask any questions."

"God!" the man sobbed. "God, I ain't tough! I'm just a punk, honest. Mister, what do you want to know? Put this fire out, and...."

Wentworth shook his head gently, "I have to conserve fuel. There's just about enough to toast you nicely." He was watching the man closely. He had no intention of letting the flames actually reach him, even though he was an ally of the Skull who had done such fearful things to Nona Malvern. He didn't think he would let the flames reach him... Smoke and burning bits of paper wafted up past the man's face.

"Gees, mister... I don't know much! I'm just here to listen in on that guy's office and his phone calls. Then sometimes the boss calls me up here, see? That's all I know, so help me God! Listen, I used to be a private dick and this guy that used to train with Whitey Hart came to me and offered me this job. Oh!"

He was straining his face away from the top of the basket, but a tongue of flame had come close enough to singe his hair. Wentworth flicked the flaming bit of paper away.

"I wouldn't want you to pass out too quickly," he said softly. "Is Whitey Hart the Skull?"

"He might be! God's truth, I don't know! I ain't never seen nobody except this guy that I'm talking about."

"His name?"

"Monk Deacon. *Oh, God....*"

Wentworth nodded. That much made sense at any rate. This was a racketeering trick with a new angle... and Hart and Deacon had been racketeers in old prohibition days. He leaned forward and cut loose the bonds that held the basket in the man's lap, set it close to the window. This ex-detective wasn't hurt, and Wentworth thought he had told all he knew. He was methodically putting out the fire in the basket when the phone bell sounded briefly!

Wentworth whirled on his prisoner. "Any password for answering this phone?" he demanded harshly—waiting.

The man seemed to be almost in a faint. He rolled his head, "Yeah. You say 'tibula and fibula!'"

The phone whined again. "Remember," Wentworth said softly. "If you're lying...."

"God, I ain't lying."

Wentworth caught up the instrument and imitated the husky tones of his prisoner.

"Okay, Barney," a man said over the wire. "Look, the boss wants to know has the Cherry Hill Hospital paid up."

Wentworth said, in a half-frightened tone, "Geez, I don't know. Look, you want to hold the wire while I see, or you want me to call you up..." He halted.

"Don't be a fool, Barney," the man said. "Look, I'll give you three minutes. When I call up, you know... see?"

Wentworth protested, but the wire went dead.

THERE WAS an intent light in his eyes. His prisoner, Barney, hadn't lied about a few things at any rate. Wentworth thought he could identify the voice over the wire as that of the ex-racketeer, Monk Deacon... and Barney wasn't supposed to know the phone number. The instant the other man disconnected, Wentworth was busy on the wire, getting in touch with an official of the phone company.

"Police business," he snapped, "and in a hurry. In three minutes, there's going to be a call come in on this wire—from criminals. I want it traced without fail. I'll call for the information."

As he hung up, he caught the rasp of a footstep behind him. He threw himself flat on the floor, rolled and snatched out his gun in a single swift movement The man, Barney, was crouched by the door... and he had his recovered gun in his fist! Even as Wentworth's eyes took in the picture, Barney fired!

Wentworth felt the shock of a bullet beneath his chest and his own automatic leaped in his fist. His lead sped true. Barney straightened under the punch of the bullet, his shoulders nailed to the wall. He drew in a slow whistling breath, then the stiffness went out of his joints. Neck, waist, knees sagged in one instant and he clattered limply to the floor.

Wentworth pushed to his feet and reached the outer door with long strides. He was ten stories up in the deserted building and unless the watchman happened to be near, it was unlikely the shots had been heard. He listened and caught the faint whine of the elevator... He shook his head. The creaking of the old cage would have blotted out the sounds. He turned back toward the office. He saw now that the basket had caused some of the torn clothing, with which he had bound Barney, to catch fire and smolder. That was how Barney had got free....

Wentworth crossed back to the desk and stood there tensely, the gun under his fist. In a few minutes. Monk Deacon would call again and at last Wentworth would have a lead to the Skull! Heaven grant that it would be in time! There still was the problem of Beck's guilt or innocence. It would have to wait. Ram Singh could hold him prisoner... He caught the sound of an opening elevator door, but it was remote. That might well be Ram Singh and Beck arriving now. Wentworth whipped up the ear-phones which connected with the dictograph upstairs.

At first, there was only silence and then the rasp of a key unlocking the door, then Beck's voice: "Lord almighty, look at all the mail! I must be getting popular as hell all of a sudden."

Ram Singh's voice lifted inquiringly, *"Sahib?"*

"Hey, Ram Singh," Beck cried. "Look, this damned mail comes from a flock of drugstores, and... Good Lord! Money! Wads of it! What in the hell...."

Wentworth was frowning with concentration. People were rarely able to dissemble with their voices. They depended more on facial expression... and he couldn't see Beck's face. Surprise and bewilderment were in his voice, no question of that. Was Beck a clever enough actor to accomplish that? Certainly, if guilty, he had known what awaited him here; would have had plenty of time to prepare his role....

The sharp ring of the phone broke in on his thoughts and he caught it up, spoke the formula into the mouthpiece.

"What's the dope on the hospital?" Monk Deacon's voice demanded.

"They paid," Wentworth answered, still in Barney's hoarse voice. "Geez, this is a sweet racket. I never saw so much dough! There must be a thousand letters up in that guy's office!"

"Don't try nothing, punk!" Monk rasped. "You finger any of that dough and the boss will hang you up like he done that girl."

Wentworth broke into protestations, but the click of disconnection cut him short. He'd been trying to stall, to gain the phone company as much time as possible… His thoughts flew to the mention of the hospital. Good Lord, were they on the racket list, too? The horror that could be wrought in a hospital by poisoned medicines was almost too awful to contemplate! The Cherry Hill was one of the largest private institutions in the city. Rapidly, he called the phone official.

"The call was traced all right," the official told Wentworth. "It was a new installation. A private phone in the office of the president of the Guaranteed Drug Company on Third Avenue. Yes, sir, I can give you the name of the president. Here it is… Robert Forbes."

WENTWORTH THANKED the man and deliberately replaced the phone in its cradle. Forbes, who had been a guest in his home no later than last night, who had given his prisoner a "new restorative" just before the man died… Yet it seemed madness that the man should use a private phone, listed in his own name, to make an incriminating call. But there was no time to waste in speculation. He thought that a personal call on

Forbes was indicated. Wentworth's lips stretched thin. It was a devious trail he had to follow.

Wentworth snapped up the phone again and called police headquarters, got put through to Kirkpatrick, to whom he rapidly detailed his discoveries in Beck's office and in the room below.

"The Spider was here ahead of me, Kirk," Wentworth said rapidly. "There is a dead man with the seal on his forehead. A plant here might learn something. Beck? I don't know, Kirk. He seemed genuinely surprised at the sight of all this mail. No, it wasn't addressed to him personally, but to the Pharmaceutical Protective Association, with his office number." Wentworth hesitated over mention of the drug company which Forbes headed. There might be things to accomplish there with which police might interfere. But if the Spider went there alone... and failed?

"Kirk," Wentworth interjected slowly, "I think it might be a good idea to check on the Guaranteed Drug Company, Robert Forbes, president. No, I won't be here when you arrive. I'll leave Beck under guard of Ram Singh... No, not a word about Nita or from her. I... don't know, Kirk."

He hung up the phone and for a moment longer he sat there with his lean, sensitive hands resting limply on the desk. It had been a sorry day for Nita when they had met. Since then, her life had been harassed by violence, endangered again and again. She had been tortured... Wentworth's hands flattened tautly on the desk and he pushed himself to his feet. He paused a moment over the man he had killed, to imprint the seal of the Spider. At every opportunity he must so mark the men of the Skull. The danger to himself did not matter. The Skull must learn to fear that seal....

Action now....

Seconds later, he was thrusting open the door of Beck's office. Ram Singh pivoted lithely, hand flitting toward a knife-hilt. Beck stood rigidly at the entrance of the inner office. He stepped forward immediately.

"Mr. Wentworth," he said hoarsely, "I swear to you that I know nothing of these letters or why they were sent here. I know that's hard to believe."

Wentworth nodded curtly. "Fortunately for you," he said, "I found a dictograph planted in your office and discovered that your phone has been tapped. The plant is downstairs. Unfortunately for you, the Spider has found this out also. He may hunt you up to ask some questions."

Beck's jaw jutted out and his fists knotted at his side. "I hope he does," he said fiercely. "But how do you know the Spider has been here?"

Wentworth's smile turned grim. "The Spider usually leaves a calling-card," he said quietly. "There's a dead man down there with his seal. Never mind that now. Listen. I want you, Beck, to take up that plant downstairs and receive in-coming phone calls, if there are any. Try to get a line on whoever calls. Ram Singh will stay here with you in case there's an attack... or the Spider returns!" Wentworth put his eyes on the dark gaze of the Sikh, and switched abruptly to Punjabi. "This man," he said steadily, "may be one of the vermin we hunt. I expect him to desert his post and perhaps go to his masters. Allow him to do this... but follow."

Ram Singh's teeth flashed amid his thick beard and he salaamed, cupped hands to his forehead. *"Han, sahib,"* he rumbled.

THE TAXI that sped Wentworth across the quiet city seemed barely to crawl. He had determined an open invasion of the Guaranteed Drug Company. There was a good chance that Forbes would be on hand, in spite of the fact that it was Sunday, since the police had ordered tests of all drug supplies in the city....

He found a watchman on duty at the entrance of the drug company's building, whose dust-filmed doors opened under the shadow of the Third Avenue elevated structure. There was a little delay and then Forbes himself came striding to fling the doors open for Wentworth. A frown marked his forehead and his eyes, blue behind rimless glasses, were puzzled. His white laboratory jacket was stained.

"Come in—come in, Wentworth," he said. "I didn't see how it could be you, but the watchman swore he had the name right. Is anything wrong? Can I do anything for you?"

"I hope so," Wentworth told him, his eyes secretly studying the angular lines of the man's florid face. "I want to open a dispensary for pure drugs... a place where the people can come and be sure their medicines won't be poisoned while this mad slaughter keeps up. I heard by accident that you had left Wister...."

"That would be splendid." Forbes' face glowed. "I think I can guarantee the drugs. So far, we've found nothing wrong at all… This job developed most unexpectedly. I had been approached about it soon after I went with Wister, but I didn't think much about it. When all this trouble broke, the owners thought this would be a good chance to get started. They were pretty sure of their supplies and thought that if we would guarantee them, we could get established almost over night."

They were lurching upward in the creaking elevator. "Shall we go to my lab?" Forbes asked.

Wentworth's lids drooped over his eyes. Was this a deliberate attempt to lead him away from the office where the phone was? He said, "If you don't mind, let's go where we can sit down. If your lab is like most of them, I won't find those confounded stools very comfortable. And I'm a little tired. Had you heard? The criminals… kidnapped Nita last night"

"My God, no," Forbes cried, and his concern seemed genuine. "How did it happen? Was—was Miss Moulin…."

Wentworth told him steadily while he fought with a feeling of fresh bewilderment. He could find no flaw in Forbes' behavior, and the office when they entered it was empty and unsuspicious, a barren cubbyhole boxed off at one side of a loft floor.

"Who are the owners of this concern?" Wentworth asked casually.

Forbes shook his head. "That's one thing that made me hesitate over the job," he said. "I don't know. A lawyer, Oscar Downey, made the contact; said he had full powers. Downey is reputable enough, God knows."

Wentworth nodded in slow agreement, abruptly made up

his mind. His eyes keenly on Forbes face, he said steadily, "I lied about my reason for coming here, Forbes. The truth is that phone calls from the Skull have been traced to your private telephone here."

Forbes said, stuttering, "What… the Skull? My God, Wentworth, you must be wrong." He swiveled in his chair and stared at the telephone. "Damn it, man, it just isn't possible,"

"There's no mistake, Forbes."

"But, for God's sake, you can't suspect me! Why, damn it, Wentworth…."

"How well do you know the building?" Wentworth interrupted. "The phone doesn't have to be used from your office. The wires could be tapped."

Forbes face grew grim, and there was an angry squint to his eyes. He reached for the phone. "I don't know a damned thing about the building, but we'll get the police here and find out."

"If the phone is tapped…" Wentworth said softly.

Forbes swore and his hand flinched away from the instrument. "You mean they'd overhear what I say? I don't know much about this wiretapping business. But we've got to do something, Wentworth. We can't just sit here, and…."

WENTWORTH'S MIND was filled with racing thoughts. If Forbes were giving a truthful account of the way in which things had happened, it would help to clear Beck also. But there was a more important inference. This gaunt, half-empty building might well conceal one of their hideouts. It might even be the spot in which… in which Nita was held captive. This building was not far from the scene of her kidnapping. He rose steadily to his feet.

"Can you use a gun?" he asked. "Have you got one?"

Forbes shook his head, his eyes widening. "Hell, no. I haven't had a revolver in my hands a half-dozen times in my life. You mean you… you want to check up on this alone, now?"

Wentworth briefly touched the automatics under his arms. "I think that would be an excellent idea," he said steadily. "We have only to trace the wires of your phone. Usually, they would run down the elevator shaft to the basement and connect there with the underground trunks. I think… the basement is indicated!"

Forbes jerked to his feet, "I have a half dozen men working here, and…."

Wentworth shook his head, "Just you and I, Forbes."

Forbes said violently, "You still suspect me, damn it, and… Oh, very well. I can't blame you, I suppose. But you're used to this sort of thing and I'm not." He mopped his forehead. "Frankly, I'm afraid as hell of guns. I've seen what they can do to people."

Wentworth said nothing, but gestured toward the door and Forbes stalked out ahead of him. The man was not feigning about his fear, but whether he dreaded what would be found, or whether he had told the truth about guns, Wentworth could not discern. He took the control of the elevator and kept his eyes on the phone wire cable as the cage slid downward—but he did not neglect to watch Forbes. The chemist stood firmly, but his lips were pale and now and again he mopped his forehead. He grinned, sickly.

"This is nonsense," he said, "but I am afraid."

Wentworth shook his head. "That's nothing to apologize for. You show intelligence."

The cage reached the bottom of the shaft and there still had been no break in the phone wires. At Wentworth's gesture, Forbes threw the doors wide and stepped out hesitantly. They found a light switch but it illuminated only two widely-spaced dim bulbs.

Wentworth took out his powerful miniature flashlight and laid its beam upon the phone wires. There was an automatic in his other hand as he moved rapidly along the course the line followed. His footfalls were soft and his eyes swept ceaselessly over the shadowed basement. The steam pipes made grotesque shadows against the walls. The place was thick with dust that rose in slow eddying swirls where they walked, hazed and dimmed the lights.

Forbes said suddenly, "The wires go into the wall there, and we still haven't found any tap."

Wentworth's lips were grim. Instead of being relieved, Forbes should be frightened. If there was no tap, it meant that the phone was used in Forbes office. He stood motionless and sent the lens-focused beam of his light questing over the wall. It was an ancient foundation, made of gray stone and white-washed at some remote time.

Wentworth muted his voice, "This steam installation is comparatively recent. I'm sure this building used a furnace at one time, so there will be a sub-basement. A trapdoor...."

The voice that now spoke seemed to come from a half-dozen

directions at once. It echoed in the close, thick walls of the basement and it was mocking, cold, rasping.

"Precisely, gentlemen," it said. *"There is a trapdoor, but I'm afraid you gentlemen won't find it!"*

WENTWORTH WHIRLED about, the muzzle of his gun questing like a dog's nose after a scent. At first, he could see nothing. The beam of his light was turned back by the haze of dust… or was it dust? Abruptly, Wentworth realized that there was vapor crawling toward them over the floor, a brownish ugly vapor the color of the dust, but strangely menacing in its silent approach. *It was gas!* Even as he grasped the import of that vapor, the lights flicked out!

In the same moment, ghastly figures began to lift out of that rolling cloud of gas… skeleton men with that horrid greenish glow to delineate their bones; skulls that gaped in fleshless mocking grins.

"Quickly," Wentworth snapped at Forbes, locking his left hand about the man's arm. "Back to the elevator. Don't mind those confounded figures. They're just decoys! Fakes!"

He was thrusting Forbes toward the elevator. The ghostly figures were between them and escape, but Wentworth ignored that… rushed straight toward them. He held his gunfire. What use to fire at these fake figures? He brushed past one… and the glowing bony arm swept toward him. Wentworth felt the swish of a club past his head! At point-blank range, Wentworth fired… and nothing happened. Nothing save that the figure whirled and came after him.

Wentworth fought with a sense of utter unreality, and an

unreasoning dread that shook his heart. Forbes, he realized, was screaming. The sound seemed strangely thin and inadequate… like the muted squeal of a trapped rabbit. Another figure loomed ahead and Wentworth tried to jerk up his gun. His arm seemed leaden. He suddenly couldn't feel the gun in his hand at all. Then he knew the truth. The gas was beginning to take effect! He tried to shout a warning to Forbes but somewhere in the past few seconds he had lost his grip on the chemist's arm. He could not see.

Stubbornly, Wentworth plunged on. The feeling had gone from his feet now. Something struck him heavily on the chest. Why… good God, he was on the floor! He had fallen! He pushed at it with hands and knees that registered nothing at all of sensation. He could no longer even see the macabre skeleton figures. The blackness crept inside his brain. He thought wildly that he had been right. He had found the lair of the Skull… and his very boldness had trapped him. Forbes, the cowardly one, had been right… Wentworth heard laughter, wild and mocking laughter, and realized it came from his own lips. It was the last thing he heard before the darkness exploded.

CHAPTER 9
THE EMBRACE OF DEATH

IN THE lightless room with stone walls where Nita van Sloan was held prisoner, she heard dimly the rumble of passing trains and that was the only sound to break the locked underground silence of her dungeon. She had seen no one since, hours ago, a man masquerading in the gallant robes of the Spider had thrust her into this cell.

Nita blamed herself bitterly for her capture. She knew that the fact was being used as a club over Dick Wentworth's head; and that he would defy the Skull. She had warned the Skull of this… and been laughed at. Heavens, how many hours had it been since she had left her home with the escort of police who accused her of murder?

The attack had been sharp and over almost as it began. Two cars had crowded up beside the police car and Nita, glimpsing the caped and masked figure in one of them, had thought that it was Wentworth himself who came to the rescue. When she knew the truth—when bullets had burned down the police—it was too late to do anything except submit. She paced her small prison and wrung her hands. Anything would be better than this waiting in ignorance of what had happened to Dick….

Nita stopped abruptly as one of those awful skeleton figures began to glow against her door. The portal had not opened, but there the thing stood. The gaping empty jaws moved and a croaking voice rasped at her.

"Leave this cell," it ordered. "The Master will speak to you!"

That was all.

Nita shuddered at the grisly thing but, as the figure faded from sight, she moved hesitantly toward the door. It swung wide and, outside in the corridor, were more of those horrid skeleton figures. The glow from their bones was the only light… but it glinted on revolvers in the fleshless hands! Nita had to remind herself that this was all trickery, intended basically to hide the identity of the men who confronted her. It was hard to keep herself convinced. While she stumbled along the pitch-black corridor, as directed, the creatures moved after her. There was a musty odor of decay in the air and… God in heaven! There was the dry clatter of bones as the *things* paced after her!

Nita stilled her rising hysteria and lifted her head proudly. She was the mate of the Spider. Such obvious trickery could not frighten her. Her heart thudded violently in her breast and her throat was dry… She would not be afraid. Whatever the Skull wanted with her, she would not yield!

Nita was aware presently that the close walls had opened from about her for the dry rasping of bones was no longer close and confined. Hard fingers gripped her shoulders and a gasping cry rose to Nita's lips. She fought it back as she was thrust down into a chair and ropes bit into her tender woman's flesh. Afterward, the fantastic figures went away and Nita sat in darkness, waiting… for what she could not guess. She closed her eyes and fought for the courage she knew she would need.

Moments dragged past in utter black silence and once more Nita felt hysteria rising within her. She sank her teeth into her lips… and then a *presence* forced itself into her consciousness. Her eyes flew wide and she choked down a cry. The Skull was before her!

Nita knew that instantly though it was the first time the apparition had appeared before her eyes. It was a face much more ghastly than any skull, for the flesh adhered to the very bone and the lips shrank back from long, bestial teeth. When it spoke, the jaws moved and the greenish light made writhing shadows across the face of the Skull.

"Woman, if you answer certain questions," the voice came, rusty and harsh, "I shall permit that you be killed before the flesh is stripped from your delicate bones. Otherwise, it shall be done *while you still live!*"

NITA SHUDDERED, as much at the fearful tones of the voice as at the torture which it threatened—but her head was still high and somehow she achieved a smile. She made no other answer. Death and the threat of death was no new thing to Nita van Sloan. She had one hope that buoyed her through every trial… and if that hope was destroyed, somewhere she would find courage. The utmost that death could inflict upon her was the fact that she would never see again the man she loved. *Never…* Nita drew in a quivering breath. The disembodied face before her was staring with burning eyes, the lips parted and a rasping sound of laughter came forth.

"Yes, yes, I know you have courage, my dear," it said. "But why waste courage on me? I feel nothing. I am only a brain. It will cost me nothing whether you suffer or die painlessly. The information is not even particularly important, but it will make a few things easier for us. Already, we can enter Wentworth's fortress at any time we wish. If he is not already in our power, he will be within a short while. So… I shall ask you a few questions."

Nita lifted her eyes above the mountebank skull, but she could not close her ears to that croaking voice. The Skull was so sure. His words dripped like corroding acid on her courage, insidious. It was not a chance to live he offered her; that she would have instantly rejected as a lie. But a chance to die painlessly… Nita's breast lifted with a quick breath. It was madness to hope that Dick would come. She could not even guess whether he had found the handkerchief clue or, if he had, whether the number that the druggist had called would be of any importance. This time, Dick must fail her; he who had never failed… God, how could he find her here?

"No doubt you still hope for rescue." The Skull's voice dropped to a harsh whisper. "It would be pleasant, wouldn't it, for your lover to leap from some dark corner now to challenge me? But it would be only a challenge, woman. He cannot harm me. And my men…" He laughed harshly, and in the darkness about him, there was other rasping laughter. Figures glowed against the black wall that pressed close to Nita, the glowing bones of men. Nita shuddered and there was a sagging weight in her breast.

"I have arranged for you, woman," the voice went on, "a little demonstration of what you presently will face. This woman you shall see has not harmed me, nor has the child. But her husband was a fool and would have talked to this same lover of yours. Others must learn what it is to defy the Skull. Hard, you think? Ah, but effective. Yes, yes, effective…."

The voice died out on Nita's ears and suddenly there was light in the room. Not where Nita sat but there across the room brightness shone like spotlights upon a stage. It was empty now, that stage, save for a coffin-like box of iron that stood in its midst.

Nita shuddered and closed her eyes. She knew the torture

devices of medieval barbarity all too well and what she saw was a modern "iron-maiden." Once, hapless persons had been shut in those coffins of steel, lined with fearful spikes that pierced… In spite of herself, Nita stared again at the gruesome thing. There were no spikes inside this cage, but that very fact made it more ominous. For there were pipes leading into it, and valves. What was it the Skull had threatened to *"strip the flesh from your delicate bones."*

Nita tried to steel herself for the ordeal that lay before her. She tried to hope… Instead, she prayed that Wentworth would not plunge into this fearful place. Men whom bullets could not harm… But that was madness! These were mortal beings and those skeleton silhouettes were trickery! No, while she could not see them, Nita could believe that. When they shone, horrible in the darkness, her certainty… wavered.

Abruptly, Nita jerked taut against her ropes. A man—it must be a man—had bounded into sight there beneath the spotlights. He was a grotesque thing, a dwarfed and twisted monstrosity of humanity with a great idiot's head and bandy limbs. He turned his head and blinked out into the darkness toward her and Nita could see saliva wet his lips. The dwarf capered lovingly about the iron maiden there on the stage, stroking it with misshapen hands, caressing the valves and pipes. He skipped out of sight and, moments later, he returned. This time, he was not alone. Behind him, her wrists chained together, he dragged a woman! **APATHY HAD** held Nita prisoner there in her chair but now she began to struggle. She groped for the strands of rope that bound her. Hopeless. It was certainly hopeless, but she would try… The woman there on the stage seemed without animation, without strength. The dwarf handled her like a toy. With a quick swing upon the wrist-chains, he whirled her into the gaping upright iron maiden! The woman's weight must have tripped some spring devices, for as her body struck the back of the box, metal straps snapped shut about her, holding her a prisoner, irrevocably. The dwarf capered….

"You see, woman." It was the Skull's voice, behind Nita now. "You see, there is no hope."

"Please," Nita whispered. "Oh, please. This is not necessary. Free her! I… I will answer your questions!"

The dwarf stopped before the woman. With a single claw-like movement of his hands, he ripped off her clothing. For the first time, the woman's lethargy faded. She stared about as if she awoke from some awful dream….

"But you see," said the Skull, "that is not in the bargain. This woman must die. This is merely by way of demonstration. You may earn yourself an easy death, no more than that. But it will have to be soon. I have an *errand* at certain hospitals…."

Nita was struggling fiercely, and she knew futilely, against her ropes. "In heaven's name!" she cried. "Don't do this awful thing! If you free her, I'll talk! If you kill her, nothing—you understand me, *nothing*—will make me talk!"

There was no answer from the Skull. The dwarf swung shut the iron maiden. There was a collar that fitted tightly about the woman's throat. Her head was visible, nothing more.

"You see?" The Skull's voice was a murmur. "We must make it possible for her to be identified… *afterward.*"

Nita tore at the ropes until the blood oozed from beneath her finger-nails. But her bonds did not yield at all. The dwarf stood motionless beside the torture cage, hand upon a valve while his great luminous eyes prodded out into the darkness, blinking.

"No, no," Nita cried. "In heaven's name, is there nothing that will save her?"

"Nothing," sighed the Skull. "Very well, Mignonette."

The dwarf yelped in high laughter and twisted the valve....

Sometime during the tearing horror of the minutes that followed, Nita swooned. Even in the black shadows into which her soul plunged, it seemed to Nita afterward that she could still hear those... those *screams*. And when she shuddered back to consciousness, the rasping voice of the Skull, as unemotional as Death, was sounding in her ears again.

"Woman, which shall it be?" it said. "Will you enter the embrace of Mignonette's love, with these questions answered, mercifully dead... or will you delight Mignonette's ears with your screams?"

Nita forced up her head and stared unseeingly before her. She was aware of the dread machine there with its pitiful prey, but her eyes went beyond. "Dick," she whispered. *"Dick!"* And there was no answer. There could be no answer... Her head sagged again.

"Answer, woman!" commanded the Skull. "The choice is yours!"

Nita somehow voiced words, "These questions...."

"The secrets of your lover's fortress, woman," the Skull rasped. "Already, we can open the gates, but there are still a few things we need to know. It will make a good stronghold for us when, presently, Wentworth is removed."

Nita's head came up proudly, "Are you so sure, fool?" she said clearly. "Do you think a mountebank and his fool can master him?" Somehow, she managed a ghost of laughter. "You choose your questions badly. *I will not answer them!*"

The Skull breathed a name, "Mignonette! Mignonette, she mocks us, I think!"

The dwarf capered toward Nita and, somewhere near, a bell whirred softly. She heard the Skull's muted voice.

"Woman, I shall need you no longer. The Spider has walked into our trap! He is prisoner!" He laughed again, until the harsh sound of it beat back from the walls, until it seemed to rasp within Nita's own skull. It cut off sharply... and she knew that the Skull had gone. Before her grimaced and capered the dwarf, Mignonette, and there was greediness in his luminous eyes!

NITA SHRANK as his hands touched her in the darkness, as ropes began to fall away from her. She gathered her body together. Now was her chance. She was alone with this misshapen monster. When the last ropes fell free... Hope began to thrill through her. If she could only get hold of a weapon! But she needed no weapons against this small, misshapen creature. She was thankful that, long ago when first she had joined her life with Dick's he had compelled her to learn *jiu-jitsu.*

The ropes fell and, with a bound, Nita was out of the chair. Before she had fairly gained her feet, a hand closed about her ankle and Nita pitched headlong. A weight fell upon her shoulders and gouging knees drove out her breath. Half-stunned by the fall, she felt her hands knotted together behind her back and she was lifted bodily into the air!

"Ah, no, pretty one," whispered the dwarf and his breath was nauseous against her face. "Ah, no! You think because Mignonettes is a cripple he is weak. You are wrong, pretty one!"

Without apparent effort, the dwarf swung Nita clear of the ground and, holding her above his head, ran toward the torture machine on the brilliantly lighted stage. Nita kicked out fiercely, trying to beat at that misshapen body, to batter that swollen head her knees—but it availed her nothing. She was thrown viciously to the ground and the strength went out of her. When, finally, she could struggle to her knees again, the iron maiden was empty and its shining metal arms were opened to embrace her!

The dwarf bent over her, smirking. "Ah, pretty one, it is not too late. But be kind to Mignonette...."

He laughed.

Nita gathered her forces and staggered to her feet. As the dwarf leaped toward her, she fell backward and lashed out with both heels together. It was all she could do. It was her final effort... and it failed.

The dwarf skipped aside as nimbly as a goat and, an instant later, Nita felt herself on her feet, reeling backward. Her eyes widened with horror as she realized the meaning of that. She tried to catch herself... and steel bands snapped shut about her, bands whose touch burned through her clothing. She was in the iron maiden! She shrank back from them and they only closed more tightly about her... In front of her helpless body, the dwarf danced and sang a song in a cracked, thin voice hatefully like a child's.

"You can mock me, pretty one," he sang, "but no one mocks my lovely maiden. No one can resist her embrace. No one...."

He stood before her, head cocked on one side. His clawed hands reached out to her, and Nita closed her eyes. She could do no more. She knew briefly the violence of those clutching hands and then—the door of the iron maiden clanged shut! The collar closed tightly about her throat! Nita's teeth clamped on her lip. Somewhere she must find the courage to endure this. It could not last for long. Not long... Hysteria corded her lovely throat. Her bound fists clenched behind her, pressed nails into flesh. She could hear the thud of the dwarf's quick, dancing feet, his cracked, crooning voice.

Almost against her will, Nita's eyes flared open. The valve... The dwarf toyed with it. He polished it with his strange, child-sized hands that were so incredibly powerful. He glanced up at her slyly and chuckled, set his shoulders to untwist the stubborn wheel of the valve. Nita drew on the last reserves of her strength, lifted up her eyes... and nothing happened. The dwarf laughed and he was dancing around her again, tormenting her spirit. Nita felt her courage sag. She couldn't stand much more. God, anything would be kinder! Even death by that awful pain that would come at her through the hissing pipes!

A frantic hope began to swell in her breast. The Skull had said that Dick was captured... but the Skull had not returned! Was it possible that somewhere behind these thick underground walls, Dick was fighting successfully? If only she could gain a little time! This fiend delighted in tormenting her. If he thought that she was suffering, he would delay the actual release of that valve for a little while… for a few heartbeats of time until he tired of the fun. Nita began to rail at him, to plead with him. When next he gripped the valve, she begged him to turn it open.

"Let me die now!" she panted at him. "Anything is better than this uncertainty!"

Her voice rose thinly, as if broken by terror. The delighted dwarf pretended once more to open the valve, watched her head strain back as she set her body for the torture… and he didn't open the valve. How long could she hold him like this? How long had this mad play been going on? Minutes dragged past without end, and the dwarf was tiring of his fun. He stood and watched her with those bright, blinking eyes, head cocked on one side.

She whispered, "Dick…."

Glass crashed somewhere. It sounded almost as if it were in this very room! Nita stared out into the darkness. No, she was mad. It could mean nothing to her, nothing at all. It was a trick of her disordered nerves. Dick couldn't… A glad cry burst from Nita's lips. The dwarf at her side snarled, seized the valve… and out of the roof of that pit of darkness before the stage a spear of gun-flame thrust!

As if in a dream, Nita saw the misshapen body of the dwarf plucked up by a bullet and hurled kicking to the platform. She saw a man leap down where the back-glow of the lights reached, springing from an overhead trapdoor. Nita cried out. She thought she cried out a name. It was a whisper, *"Dick!"*

Darkness swooped down upon her.

CHAPTER 10
VICTORY—AND DEFEAT

SAGGING INTO a merciful unconsciousness, Nita did not see the second man drop through the ceiling trap door, nor watch the two struggle toward her as if they fought their way through swift, deep water. They moved side by side with a heavy slowness, holding their guns far out and carefully so that they could see them—side by side, Richard Wentworth and Donald Beck!

"You keep watch," Wentworth said thickly. "You got less gas. Gun faster." He reached the iron maiden and began to fumble with the clasps. "It's all right, Nita. All right now!"

She heard that.

He was frantic with the need for haste, but all his movements were made with wooden limbs. At last the clips of the iron maiden swung open and he could lift Nita tenderly from the torture trap. He gathered her torn garments about her, wrapped his coat about her shoulders and swung her up in his arms.

Safe....

Nita was stirring faintly now. "Oh, Dick," she whispered. "The Skull said you were trapped."

"I was," Wentworth told her thickly. "They were keeping their distance and letting the gas do their work. Then Beck came in and dragged me out. He got a dose of gas doing it. I don't know why the Skull's men haven't followed to finish us off. Two of us, and both groggy with gas. I...."

A slashing beam of light knifed down from the trapdoor and Wentworth painfully lifted his gun. A man's voice called down to him cheerfully, "It's the police, Mr. Wentworth. Where are the rats? We can't find them!"

It was a matter of minutes then before they could be drawn up through the trapdoor and taken to the open air. An intern made a rapid examination and his report.

"The gas has strained your heart, sir," he told Wentworth. "The best thing you can do is to go to the hospital for a long rest."

Wentworth smiled at him wryly, "That's the best, is it, Doctor? How bad is that strain?"

The intern shook a worried head, "I'd have to run a cardiograph to tell that, sir, but there's a definite disturbance. Frankly, it may be very serious."

Wentworth shrugged. He still couldn't make his words come quickly, but his brain seemed supernaturally keen. "I think," he said carefully, "that is an effect of the gas that will wear off when it's completely out of my system."

"A stimulant then," the man suggested.

He started to prepare a hypodermic needle and Wentworth's eyes fell on the ambulance name-plate, *Cherry Hill Hospital*. A startled oath leaped to his lips. In the rush of violent action he had forgotten the phoned inquiry of the Skull about that very hospital! He had assured the Skull that the hospital had paid, but by now the Skull must know that was trickery. He gripped the intern's arm.

"Never mind that injection," he said, with something like his own crispness. "When you return to the hospital, insist on poison tests being run on every drug in the place. It's been threatened by the Skull."

He whirled toward the police officers, glimpsed Ram Singh in the background. He was understanding things more clearly now. Plainly, Beck had been suspicious of him and had followed for that reason. Ram Singh had pursued Beck and had summoned the police for safety. Certainly, he could no longer suspect Beck since the man had saved his life at the risk of his own!

Nita touched Wentworth's arm. "I remember now," she said, her voice low with anxiety. "The Skull said he had 'an errand to do' at some hospitals!"

Wentworth nodded. "I'll get hold of Kirkpatrick right away."

He moved on heavy feet toward a cigar store where he could reach a telephone. God, what horror the poisons of the Skull would wreak in the hospitals of the city! What in heaven's name could the man expect to gain from such practices? Surely, he did not hope to collect racket money from hospitals? Almost, it seemed the man must be killing for sheer love of slaughter!

WENTWORTH TRIED to hurry and an overwhelming weakness made him stagger as he moved. There was squeezing pain around his heart, physical this time and he clutched his breast. His head sagged as he pushed into the store. His lips twisted bitterly with the realization that he dared not allow a stimulant to be used. That was the horror that was at work throughout the city. At one stroke, the Skull had nullified all

131

the years of medical research and science. Worse than that, he had turned those discoveries into torture potions for humanity!

He phoned his warning to Kirkpatrick, told him with difficulty of the battle in the drug company plant. "Forbes was with me when the Skull attacked," he said heavily, "but disappeared during the gas. Your men are hunting the Skull's gang, but so far without success. They apparently had some secret exit from the plant God alone knows what is coming next... Yes, I'll be at my home if you want me."

Wentworth made his slow way then to the Daimler, which Ram Singh had driven, and he and Nita started home with Beck. Wentworth felt incredibly feeble and a fear was gnawing at his heart... a new and strange thing for the Spider! Suppose the young intern was right and his heart was permanently strained! There was an end of all his crusades, the end of everything... With heavy hands, Wentworth opened a compartment in the car and drew out the first-aid kit. It had been all right when he had used it on the poisoned child, he recalled. Nita took it from his fumbling hands and rapidly fixed it, gave Wentworth the shot. It helped.

Wentworth leaned back against the cushions and began to talk. "Beck, I am sure now that you know nothing of those racket payments you received. The police will be harder to convince, but perhaps it can be arranged. Nita, you received no intimation of the real source of income of the Skull, did you?"

Nita replied softly in the negative. Her eyes were anxious on Wentworth's leaden face. Her fingers clung to his arm.

Beck said urgently, "But there has to be some monetary reason behind all this! The Skull isn't just murdering for the fun of it."

Nita shuddered a little, remembering the emotionless mockery of that voice. It was conceivable, since she had seen and heard him.

Wentworth shook his head. "It may be," he said, "that Forbes' drugs are unadulterated and that, whether he is himself innocent or guilty, the Skull owns that company—hopes to cash in heavily when his company is proved sound. That would augur tremendous profits. Once the firm was established, it would take the other companies years to restore their credit with the public. It could be a move to drive down the value of drug stocks. God knows, they'll be down practically to zero when the market opens in the morning...."

Wentworth's eyes opened keenly, "How do you feel, Beck?"

"I'm all right," Beck said sturdily, "I didn't get much of a dose of that gas."

Wentworth nodded. "I haven't any doubt at all that selling orders on drug stocks are deluging the Wall Street offices right now. Now, if we could find a few who were ordering *purchases* of drug stocks!"

Beck said softly, "By God, Mr. Wentworth, I believe you've got something there. Say the word and I'll get down to the financial district. If there's heavy trading threatening tomorrow, the telegraph people will have notified the brokers at their homes. I'll wager there will be staffs at work, getting ready for tomorrow."

"The police are going to be on your trail, Beck," Wentworth

reminded him. "The only reason you weren't arrested at the Forbes plant was because no general alarm has been put out yet and those men didn't know you were sought. I'll do what I can to stave it off, but I don't know... You can't give much explanation of that racket money pouring into your office."

"None at all!" Beck said stubbornly. "They'll have to believe me, sir... Let me out at that subway station, and I'll shoot downtown. You'll be at home?"

Wentworth nodded and signaled Ram Singh to stop the car. "Good luck, Beck." He offered his hand. "I won't forget what I owe you."

Beck's square-cut face flushed a little. "Forget it, sir," he said, and swung out of the car.

Nita waved to him as the Daimler surged forward again, then she settled down comfortably beside Wentworth and took his lean, powerful hand in both of hers. There was a cold fear within her, too, for this brave man beside her. The doctor's words had frightened her terribly. He might be mistaken, of course. Once they were safe home... Rigidity crept along her nerves and Wentworth's head swung toward her.

"What is it, Nita?"

"I just remembered," she said. "Oh, the Skull may have been lying, but he said... that he could enter your home at any time he wanted. He said, they knew how to get in."

"Tell Ram Singh to hurry," Wentworth said quietly.

He lifted his heavy hands and took hold of his automatics, looked down at their precise, perfectly functioning mechanism. As long as there were bullets in their clips and fingers to pull them, they would work perfectly. No heart in *them* to give out. Wentworth's lips pulled into a straight, thin line. Rest, the doctor had said. Rest… Wentworth laughed harshly. How could any man rest when such hell had been loosed on earth? He flicked on a short-wave radio set and heard the police announcer speeding cars to the hospitals. A sharp anxiety seized him. He switched to another channel, hunting a news broadcast.…

WITH SHOCKING suddenness, a voice blasted loudly into the tonneau. "Poison has been found in the hospital supplies of the city," the announcer said excitedly, "but not before seventeen patients had died at Cherry Hill Hospital. Four of these were undergoing emergency operations. Too late, the authorities found out that the ether had been poisoned. Three persons undergoing observation in the psychiatric ward were given quieting drugs… and instead of quieting, they turned into homicidal maniacs. One of them broke loose and reached the children's ward before he could be caught, and three of the patients there were murdered."

Nita gasped at the news. "Oh, that's horrible. Horrible! How could any human being do a thing like that!"

The announcer's magnified voice silenced her whispered words. "Two more of those poor victims of the criminals who murdered Nona Malvern have been found," he rushed on. "This time, it was the wife of a druggist and her infant son. They had been reduced to skeletons except, for the heads and faces, which were left untouched apparently so that they could be identified. There was a message attached to the skeletons:

" 'They say that women always talk and cannot keep a secret—
But it's hard to talk, or even breathe
   With no flesh on your brisket' "

Wentworth fumblingly cut off the switch. Where would all this horror end? He was forced to admit that he had accomplished painfully little against the Skull. The discovery of the racket money at Beck's office appeared to mean little; probably was intended to be revealed as a blind for the real operations of the Skull. Oh, he had succeeded in exposing one of the Skull's hideouts, but it meant so damnably little….

The car was whirling into Sutton Place now and Wentworth handed to Nita the sonic whistle which operated the gates of his home. She put it to her soft lips and her eyes were straining ahead for the first glimpse… It was reassuring to see the severely plain wall and the mansion itself rising beyond. But what would they find inside? Nita blew the curiously varying note of the sonics whistle, timing the tones carefully, and the gates slid soundlessly open. The Daimler sped through and drew to an easy halt before the doors.

Wentworth forgot his weakness and started to leap to the ground. He stumbled, caught himself only by a violent effort, and thereafter he moved more carefully. Ram Singh and Nita were at his side in an instant; then the tall Sikh strode on ahead. There was tension in the softness of his stride, in the taut roll of his heavy shoulders. He stopped and his hand pointed to a red smear on the floor!

Wentworth rasped out an oath. They pushed into the elevator together.

"They couldn't have any reason to harm Melissa," Nita whispered. "She has done nothing, nothing at all."

Her voice died as her memory swung back, flinchingly, to the Skull. The woman he had killed in that torture machine had done nothing to him either. She had only happened to be the wife of a druggist....

The elevator door slid open and Nita darted out, ran through the hallway calling to Melissa. There was no answer, but on the floor of the drawing-room was the torn fragment of a dress, and there were more of those ominous red stains. Wentworth walked heavily across the room.

"Jackson and Jenkyns," he said to Ram Singh. "They must be somewhere here."

The tall Sikh strode off silently through the house. Nita's cries echoed emptily as she still, futilely, called Melissa. Wentworth's face was bitter and grim. Perhaps they had taken Jenkyns and Jackson with them, too, to be found presently with a taunting verse pinned to their fleshless bones. And the Spider was hobbled. His hands, gripping the automatics that seemed too heavy for them, were trembling with weakness. Almost, the gallant heart of the Spider despaired. He dropped heavily into a chair. Presently, Nita came darting back into the room.

"She's gone, Dick!" Nita cried. "The Skull..." She swayed and covered her eyes with her hands. "Oh, Dick, that torture machine... The Skull forced me to watch a woman die in it." She took slow stumbling steps and slumped down on the floor, put her head against Wentworth's knees. "Oh, Dick...."

MOMENTS AFTERWARD, Ram Singh strode into the

room with the limp body of the aged Jenkyns in his arms. The Sikh's fine eyes were hot with anger. "They war on women and old men, these vermin," he said violently. "*Wah*, they are less than vermin! Lead thy servant to them, master!"

Nita drove her flagging body to her feet and bent over Jenkyns. Her voice was crisp as she issued orders to Ram Singh. "It doesn't seem too serious, Dick. He was hit over the head."

Wentworth closed his eyes and deliberately drove the horror and despair from his mind; squeezed out the last ounce of emotion. They might have crippled the Spider's body, but his brain was still painfully alive. He must revise his whole campaign against the Skull—do it swiftly and well. He lay like a dead man, his guns resting on his thighs, face drained of blood. He was like that, still unmoved, when Jenkyns aroused.

He could tell little. He had heard the sonics whistle blow in the street to open the gates and set about preparing a quick meal. Someone had slipped up behind him presently and then hit him over the head.

Wentworth's eyes flicked open. The Skull had not lied then. He had penetrated the intricate secret of the sonics whistle, timing and tones. It had to be precise or the gate would not operate. That was an amazing thing... The whir of the phone cut in on his thoughts and Jenkyns tried feebly to rise and answer it. Nita forced him to lie still and herself brought the portable instrument to Wentworth's side.

"This is Beck." The young detective sounded wildly excited. "I've only checked one office, sir, but you're right. There's a landslide of selling orders. And there are a few buying orders. One of the biggest was put in by Wilton Toley, the district attorney."

"Good work, Beck," Wentworth told him quietly. "See how many other buying orders you can find. This is important!" Wentworth was smiling as he replaced the phone in its cradle. Now he knew what to do! He began to make a series of phone calls, first to his bankers.

"Richard Wentworth speaking," he said quietly. "Orders, Henderson. Get busy at once. I'll send you an unlimited order against my cash. As soon as the markets open in the morning, start buying drug stocks. I want to corner the market. Any drug stock offered, it doesn't matter. If the cash runs out, liquidate my bonds and stocks... *but corner the market!*"

Wentworth smiled at the surprised protests over the wire. "Don't let the future of the stocks worry you, Henderson," he said. "They'll be sound enough when this terror is over. Wait... One more instruction. I want all of the purchases made in my name. Make no attempt to cover up my identity and don't withhold information if the newspapers get in touch with you. That's all. Yes, of course, I'll confirm it in writing within the hour."

Nita was staring at him without understanding as he went rapidly on with his calls, getting in touch with brokers and financial men. To each one, he gave the same order, with the same instructions, that all was to be done in his name.

"But what in the world, Dick?" Nita cried. "Every one will suspect you now! Already, a lot of blame has been put on the Spider! If you buy in these stocks..." Wentworth smiled grimly, "Yes, of course, dear. Now if you'll play at being my secretary for a while, and call a telegraph boy, we'll get out these written confirmations. They won't go the whole distance without them because they'll want proof of the orders. And I want them to go the *whole* distance!"

For a long moment, Nita stared at him. There was a question in her eyes.

Wentworth laughed, sharply. "My mind is all right, Nita," he said. "Don't worry. They've crippled the Spider's body, but they haven't stopped me yet!"

Presently the work was done and the orders dispatched by a messenger boy. It was within five minutes of that time that the signal bell of the gate sent its summons through the house. Ram Singh strode quickly to an electrical device which permitted him to see what lay outside the gate. He turned stiffly.

"The police, *sahib,*" he said softly. "Kirkpatrick *sahib* and the man, Toley. Many uniformed men."

Wentworth smiled faintly. "Very well, Ram Singh. Admit Kirkpatrick *sahib* and the man, Toley. No one else."

Nita crossed quickly to his side, "This is trouble, Dick," she said. "Stanley Kirkpatrick wouldn't come like that if it weren't, without calling you."

Wentworth pushed to his feet, put his arms about Nita. "Yes, dear," he said, "it is undoubtedly trouble. The Skull is trying his best to frame me, with Toley's help. I may have to run for it—I may."

"Not alone!" Nita cried. "Dick, you can't leave me again."

For a moment, Wentworth held her close, gazing down into her worried eyes. Then he bent and kissed her softly. He made no other answer to her cry. "Dear, will you go and play on the organ pipes… with your hands. Have the door of the secret room so that it will open at a touch."

NITA WENT swiftly and the elevator doors opened. Toley bounced out and there was triumph on his sharp, narrow face. Kirkpatrick followed him more steadily, a worried frown on his forehead. He paused just inside the door and knuckled the pointed ends of his mustache, a habit of his.

"Dick," he said quietly, "you will order Ram Singh to admit my men. I did not care to force the issue."

Wentworth shook his head. "There was no search warrant, I believe? I think we'd better let matters rest like this for the moment."

Ram Singh stood, with folded arms, just inside the room. His dark eyes glittered as they roved from his master to the two men he had admitted.

Kirkpatrick said sharply, "Dick, this is not your usual greeting."

"This is not your usual method of visiting me," Wentworth told him quietly. "My friends are always welcome. Are you my friend today, Kirk?"

Toley said shortly, "Enough of this foolishness. Arrest him, Commissioner."

Wentworth stood warily poised. The pain was in his breast again from the quickened bearing of his heart. He had guessed right then. His voice was even, sardonic. His eyebrows lifted with a quirk of mockery.

"I believe it is customary," he said gently, "for a prospective prisoner to be informed of the charges lodged against him?"

Toley braced his short, vibrant body. "Sure, I'll tell you, Mr. Spider Wentworth. There are more than a hundred counts of murder against you, signed with your own little seal. And don't think you can beat it. I've been busy today."

"Busy buying up drug stocks, Toley?" Wentworth asked gently.

Toley's face grew fiery red. "That's my business, damn it. Don't try to evade the issue. I had bullets dug out of the trees out at Wister's place and identified mine and Kirkpatrick's. The others are yours. They were fired from the same gun that killed the man at Beck's office and the man in the apartment where the druggist was killed. You killed them both, Wentworth, and you put your seal on them both."

Kirkpatrick came slowly forward, and he placed himself so that Ram Singh could not come at his back.

"Richard Wentworth, I arrest you on two charges of murder," he said, his voice stiff, emotionless. "Hand over your guns!"

In the doorway, Nita cried out sharply, "I'll shoot the first man who moves!"

CHAPTER 11
FUGITIVES

TOLEY WHIPPED around toward the door and stared, bug-eyed, at Nita with a small automatic held competently in her right hand. Ram Singh, at a word from her, laid his hand upon the handle of his great-bladed knife. Wentworth kept his sardonic smile, but there was warmth now in his heart. Nita has not seized control through any doubts of him, but to place herself definitely outside the law. Now, unless he took Nita with him, she would be arrested and jailed as his accessory. Perhaps, even that would be better....

Wentworth cut off his thoughts. There was no time to delay. He lifted his hands and drew out his guns. His arms had that same tired weakness in them, but he didn't think either of these men would know that.

"Thanks, Nita," Wentworth said quietly. "Now, take their guns and go... to the place you know. I will join you. Ram Singh, go and guard the *missie sahib.*"

Nita did as he bade her, then behind Kirkpatrick she stood to peer toward Wentworth with questioning eyes. There was doubt and fear in her glance, but Wentworth only smiled and motioned her on. "I'll be with you in a moment," he said.

Toley was ranting, but Kirkpatrick stood, stiffly indignant and silent, until Nita and Ram Singh had left the room. He was facing Dick, not ten feet away and their eyes met... and held. Kirkpatrick's eyes revealed their pain, but the set of his mouth showed no tendency to swerve from his duty.

"I'm between you and the door, Dick," he said steadily. "It is my intention that you shall face this charge of murder. I know that, innocent, you have fled the police before this in order to continue battling against criminals. Now, you have not that excuse. We have the criminals under lock and key."

Wentworth started. "What are you saying, Kirk. What criminals?"

"We will have confessions by morning," Kirkpatrick pushed on. "Beck and Forbes were in this together. We have them in prison and it is only a question of time before they tell their whole story. The evidence against both of them is too powerful for them to hope to escape."

Wentworth shrugged. "About Forbes, I don't know," he said. "Beck is innocent. There is stronger evidence against Toley here than against anyone else."

Kirkpatrick's gaze did not waver.

Wentworth said, "Ask him why he's buying drug stocks. Don't you see that all this racketeering business is a blind? It's merely to cover up the real purpose which is the wholesale purchase of drug stocks at the ridiculously low figure to which they'll drop. There can be no permanent impairment of their value, and...."

"How did those criminals know you were going to Wister's, so that they could set up that elaborate trap for you? Surely, you did not tell them. If you suspect me, remember that Toley said he would not go until the next day. Toley would have discovered which men were most likely to talk among the druggists, so he would know which needed to be silenced. He knew that Nita would be arrested, and there must have been some advance warning there or else she could not have been waylaid on the way to the police headquarters."

Toley laughed with sharp mockery. "You can't be very sure of my guilt, Mr. Spider Wentworth. I'm still alive."

144

Kirkpatrick said, "All right, Dick. I'm coming after those guns now."

"Stop, Kirk," he ordered softly.

Kirkpatrick's face tightened, but he did not check his slow stride forward. Desperation pumped at Wentworth's lungs. He could not risk a personal encounter with Kirkpatrick with his heart in this condition. If his heart did not fail, he would be so weakened as to be an easy conquest, unless… His trigger finger whitened with pressure.

"Go ahead and shoot." Kirkpatrick's face was suddenly twisted.

Wentworth squeezed the trigger. The heavy blast rolled across the room. With a scream, Toley whirled and went racing wildly out of the room. He collided with the door-jamb, fell, was up and running again in a heartbeat. He had not waited to see what happened.…

WENTWORTH HAD indeed fired, at point-blank range, but just before he squeezed the trigger, he jerked the muzzle high. In the same instant that he fired, he leaped forward. As he had known must happen, Kirkpatrick had winced and closed his eyes at the shock of that gun-blast so close to him.

Wentworth needed that instant's advantage. He swung the gun-barrel lightly at Kirkpatrick, planning to knock him out. The gun landed, but Kirkpatrick was instantly grappling with him. In his anxiety not to hurt his friend, Wentworth had miscalculated. He had not struck hard enough.

Kirkpatrick's arms were like iron bands about him and there

was no strength in Wentworth's body. "For God's sake, Dick," Kirkpatrick whispered. "Don't make me do this! Surrender!"

Wentworth wrenched, and there was no use at all. He pulled the only trick he could. He let his body go suddenly inert and sagged with all his weight against Kirkpatrick's grip. The hold did not loosen, but the commissioner was thrown off balance. As he stumbled forward, Wentworth wrenched an arm free and struck again. This time it was hard enough.

Wentworth stood, sobbing for breath, above the prone body of his friend. "I'm sorry, Kirk," he whispered. "Damned sorry, old man."

He turned away and his feet dragged. He staggered and thrust a gun-filled hand against the wall for support. There was a darkness before his eyes and helpless anger shook him. It was a vicious thing that the service to which he dedicated himself stood always between him and happiness; between him and his friend. He would never regret the service, nor his purpose, but sometimes it was hard… His left hand was pressed hard against his chest. This was the bitterest blow that any criminal ever had struck against him, to leave a man whole and unwounded and helpless….

What the hell? He was lying on the floor. Damn it, he had to get on! He began to crawl… Figures were rushing toward him. He tried to lift a gun and heard Nita calling to him, felt the strong arms of Ram Singh about him.

"Seaplane," Wentworth gasped. "Go up the Sound until it's dark, then double back to… to…."

The darkness crowded in irresistibly this time, washed over

him in waves that, presently, took on a strange rhythm. He identified it at last… It was the motor of the plane, and they were in the air. He opened his eyes and saw Nita's face.

"All right," he whispered. "It's all right now."

He slept….

WHEN WENTWORTH awoke again he was in a room he had never seen before and, moments after he opened his eyes, Nita came energetically in and bent over him. "I drugged you," she said calmly. "Otherwise, you'd have kept right on going and killed yourself. I couldn't really let you do a thing like that."

Wentworth grinned up at her. "I guess I'm relieved of command," he said. "Where are we? How much time has elapsed? What's happening?"

Nita laughed at him, and relief was apparent in her tones. "I believe you're going to be all right, Dick, as soon as the full effects of that gas have left your system. I haven't dared to have a doctor in… All right, I'm going to answer your questions. We're in North Carolina, in a tourist camp just outside Wilmington. We've been here two days. You've been awake before long enough to eat, but the drugs kept you from remembering, I guess. As for what's happening, I don't know. I haven't seen a newspaper or listened to a radio. I sent Ram Singh back to New York with the plane."

Wentworth's smile faded. "Two days," he said slowly. "God alone knows what could happen up there in this time. The police…."

"The police," Nita told him firmly, "are better able to fight the

Skull than you are—for the present. You're staying right here until you're strong—if I have to sit on you!"

Wentworth stared up at her fixedly for a moment, then smiled again as the color flooded Nita's cheeks. But his smile was a transient thing, and was replaced by that same worried frown. "You're right," he agreed, "or you would be right if it weren't for my plans. You see, I wanted the Skull to find me. He has to… and he has to take me alive, or there will be no profits for him. I have to go where he can find me."

Nita leaned over and touched a cool palm to his forehead. It was plain she did not understand.

Wentworth moved restlessly. "Don't you understand, Nita?" he asked. "If my orders have been followed out, I should have what amounts to a corner on the drug stocks, by this time. The Skull was counting on making that corner himself. The only way he can cash in on the profits of his murders now is for him to find me, alive, and force me to sign over the stocks I hold to him. When he does that…."

Nita's face was wholly grave now. "I understand, Dick. I'll get some newspapers, if you'll promise to try to sleep while I'm gone. Please try to realize, Dick. Unless you're strong, all that work will accomplish nothing at all. When—when the Skull captures you, you have to be strong enough to fight and win."

Wentworth said quietly, "I promise." He thought his mind would be too full of whirling thoughts and plans, but sleep came quickly….

When he awoke he was much stronger and the newspapers were beside him.

As he read, his face grew grim and stern. The deaths had continued to mount in New York. Drugstores, reopened after careful check on their contents, nevertheless were still found to have poison stocks. A sneak-thief, caught exchanging a poisoned bottle for an innocuous one from the stock of a store had said the Spider forced him to do it! Toley was rampant with his accusations that Wentworth was the Spider, and made the most of his evidence of the bullets. He glossed over the loophole in his structure—that he could not prove the bullets taken from the trees had come from Wentworth's guns! Nor had he stopped there. He was demanding the removal of Commissioner Kirkpatrick for allowing Wentworth to escape!

There were headlines on the stock market and editorial attacks on Wentworth for his attempts to corner the market to "reap the profits of wanton murder" as the editorials put it.

Nita came in then. "I have some of yesterday's papers, too," she said. "Both Forbes and Beck were released on writs of habeas corpus and Downey is their lawyer. Beck is saying now that he was duly elected head of the druggists' protective association and that the money in his office was their dues."

Wentworth stared at Nita, digesting that news. "He can get away with that if the druggists support him in the story," he said slowly. "And with the menace of the Skull, and what he has done to that poor woman and her child, I think the druggists will."

Nita nodded. "They already have, but I thought Beck was innocent."

Wentworth let the papers sag from his hands. "He saved my life when the Skull was trying to kill me," he said simply. "The

Skull could bring the same type of pressure to bear upon Beck. I may be wrong, but I think Beck rather went off the deep end over Melissa… and the Skull has her a prisoner. I hope… she's still a prisoner."

Nita said slowly, "I heard a radio report while I was in the city. An epidemic of typhoid has broken out in New York and the first five persons inoculated, with what they thought was typhoid vaccine, died in convulsions… *poisoned.*"

Wentworth's fists clenched whitely. He said, with effort, "Nita…."

Nita's head bowed. "Yes, Dick," she whispered. "I know you must go. But… oh, Dick, I'm afraid… afraid…."

CHAPTER 12
CAPTURED!

THE NARROW street was crowded from wall to wall with people. They stood rock-silent to listen to the hoarse-voiced man who harangued them.

"It's the fault of them bloody murderers in city hall," he bellowed. "They can get us good medicine, if they want to. All of them are getting medicine, ain't they? And what do we get? We get poison."

Another man stood below him in the car on which the speaker was perched. "Nice going, Plug," he whispered. "You got them going."

A howl from someone in the mob, "To hell with the city

bosses. Let's go tell them off. Let's go get the medicine before we're all poisoned like dogs."

Another voice took up the cry. The man called Plug looked down at his companion. "I tell you when the Skull plans a thing, it's done well—ain't it, Bumper?"

The crowd was echoing the cry now. The speaker on top the car raised both hands. "Come on, boys, I'll lead you," he shouted. "On to city hall!"

He jumped down off the car and began to stalk through the mob. People followed him. There was a low mutter of anger. It mounted like the pound of storm-driven waves, and now there was the tramp of feet, too. The mob was on the march. Beside the car where the man called Bumper stood, a number of men drew together. They were all grinning.

"It's like taking candy from a kid," one said.

Bumper nodded. "Sure. There'll be three mobs coming at city hall. The cops are sure to get wind of it and it will go on the radio. Then…."

"Then we got the Spider, eh, Bumper?"

"You said it, Whitey. You can't fool the Skull. This guy, the Spider, will come out to try to stop the mob. It's just the sort of damn fool thing he likes to do. When he does…."

They piled into the car and it pushed into the rear of the mob until it reached a corner, then circled to get ahead of the marching, shouting people. There were indignant, bitter faces in that mob. Men who had lost loved ones and others whose families were ill with diseases they dared not treat with medicines. Clubs materialized in their hands and bricks and cobbles were clenched in ugly fists. They thought they were men with a grievance, this toy mob that the Skull had blown into life.

It was another mob on another street that Donald Beck saw. He heard the angry mutter of it before he caught sight of its leading, ragged ranks. He hesitated, then ducked into a phone booth and called the police. Afterward, he trailed along in the wake of the mob. His face was pale and set when he saw the three mobs, marching from different directions, swirl into Broadway and head downtown. The buses were stopped, and cars skittered from the path of the march. Windows were smashed by quick-flung rocks.

When the mob was within four blocks of city hall, a battered small coupé swung out into the middle of Broadway from a side street and stopped. Instantly, a door opened and a man got out, climbed rapidly to the roof. He stood there then, arms uplifted in a commanding gesture. There was a long black cape swinging from his shoulders, and the wide brim of a black hat was drawn down over his eyes. His voice rolled out, powerful and deep.

"Stop this madness, men! You are being led by murderers and criminals! Stop before you are slain… *The Spider commands it!*"

At the corner beyond where the Spider had taken his stand, an automobile started out into the street, then skittered back out of sight. The men inside it burst into excited laughter.

Bumper shook his small head. "We got to take him alive. Wait."

The Spider had no guns in his hands, and his eyes were keen as they swept over the mob.

"Listen, men," he urged, his resonant voice carrying easily

through the mutter of the mob. "When have I ever lied to the people? When have I failed to serve them? I tell you that you are being used as tools by the very men who have poisoned your families!"

A young working man near the front of the mob thrust forward, shaking a club angrily. "He lies!" the man shouted. "This Spider—he is the one who killed our people. The papers say so. He is the poisoner. Lynch him. Lynch the Spider!"

For a moment, a stunned silence gripped the crowd, then the cry took hold. Everywhere, voices tossed the phrase back like echoes. "Lynch the Spider!"

Somewhere, a revolver cracked, and Wentworth heard the bullet hiss past him, but he did not flinch. Except by accident, he knew that he would not be killed. The men of the Skull would see to that. He lifted his hands to shout at the mob, and then his eyes narrowed. What he wanted was to turn aside the mob from the city hall, wasn't it? That and submit to capture by the men of the Skull?

Well, this was his chance. If they chased the Spider to lynch him, the mob would string out along the narrow side streets. Many of them would weary and turn away and there would be no one left to urge them on toward the city hall. As for the rest… the Spider would take his chances.

Wentworth began to run. It was a foolhardy thing he did and he knew it. Nita was two blocks away on a side street waiting. But he dared not lead the mob toward her car.

Abruptly, a car carrying a half-dozen men swirled into Broadway and cut down the street toward which Wentworth was

153

"Lynch the Spider!" they shouted.

heading. The Spider's taut drawn lips grimaced into a smile. If he had miscalculated now, he was finished. His guess was that those men would be the killers of the Skull. If they proved to be either the police or members of the mob....

His breath was already short when he rounded the corner with the mob in full cry behind him. A rock bounced off the pavement at his feet; another skimmed past his shoulder. Wentworth's eyes searched desperately, saw the car just ahead. He whipped out a gun, sprinted toward it. As he sprang to the running-board, he jammed the gun against the head of the driver.

"Get going, and get going fast," he ordered.

The man's face went gray. "Sure, sure," he whimpered, while he fumbled with the gear-shift. "Geez, you don't need to do that to me, Spider. Me, I drove here to save you, soon as I heard that mob yell. I think you're a swell guy. Sure, I do. Don't I, fellows?"

There were other men in the car and they all nodded hurriedly. "Sure, you do, Bumper. We all do."

One of them opened the door. "Get in, Spider."

Wentworth's face was grim as the car whipped forward.

He thrust his gun back into its holster and, at the same instant, one of the men struck him from behind. Wentworth fell limply to the floor. He heard the men burst into cackling laughter, and after that nothing for a long time....

WHEN WENTWORTH regained consciousness, it was with a rush. For moments, he could not place himself and then the darkness of the place in which he was bound, and the harsh, rasping voice he heard snapped the whole thing clearly into his mind. He swung his aching head and caught his breath.

The room in which he found himself might have been a replica of the loft building sub-basement in which he had found and rescued Nita. A pale greenish glow of light showed him that... shone, too, from the Skull that seemed to float in the darkness off to one side, whose voice had brought him back to his senses. He knew that his arms were bound painfully behind him and the pressure of his knees together revealed that they had found the hidden gun which he had hoped to use in extremity.

But it was not these things that drew the gasp of dismay from his stoical heart. Before him were two glass cases that duplicated the iron maiden he had seen before. In front of these stood a man with a flexible metal hose, a man though he seemed but a framework of glowing bones. And in those shimmering beautiful glass cases that he knew were torture coffins of death, were two women—Melissa and *Nita van Sloan!*

"So you see," the Skull was saying smoothly, "there is no hope at all, Wentworth. None at all. It was plain that you would suspect trickery, Wentworth. The guileless way in which you stepped into the car indicated that if nothing else. So we merely looked for whoever would be trailing you... and found her. A pity—yes, a pity."

Wentworth drew on all his stamina for resistance. Once he had done what the Skull would require, there could be no hope at all. There was yet a little shred of hope. He had told Nita to get in touch with Ram Singh and have him in turn trail her, but at first they had not been able to reach the Sikh. It was just possible Nita had succeeded after he left. He had wanted that double insurance passionately, but this trap had been sprung so soon after they had flown to New York that there had not been time to make sure.

"I am offering you, Wentworth," said the Skull, "the same alternative which I made to the woman. An easy death in exchange for what I wish."

Wentworth forced a smile to his lips. "It would be most unwise for you to persist in murder now, Skull," he said, "since you wish to remain incognito. Surely, you did not think that I would depend on a single trailer? The police are undoubtedly surrounding this building now...."

The Skull laughed. "If you refer to the Sikh, do not build your hopes too high, Wentworth. We contented ourselves with shooting him."

"I see," Wentworth acknowledged quietly, "and you want, of course, a transfer of my holdings in drug stocks."

Wentworth's eyes, under lowered lids, were questing over the room. His wrists were secured by ropes and other ropes bound him to a post. He was within a half dozen feet of the glass cases in which Nita and Melissa were prisoners.

Nita turned her head and smiled at him bravely. Melissa was pale, but her head was resolutely high. There was no one in sight save for this ghostly head that floated in space and the man with the flexible hose whose purpose Wentworth could guess only too well. The Skull had not had the time, or the facilities, to reconstruct his iron maiden, but he had an admirable substitute.

Wentworth said quietly, "I have more things to bargain with

than that, Mr.... *Skull.* There are certain papers on their way now to Commissioner Kirkpatrick, which could be intercepted since I asked him to hold them for me. Certain papers which contain some very fine circumstantial evidence, such as the way in which the sonics whistle that opens my gates was duplicated. Why, when so much that went on in my home was known, a certain visit made, of course, in the line of duty, was ignored by the Skull."

Behind him, he was working on the bonds frantically. If he could only wet the ropes, he thought he might succeed in stretching them enough... just enough.

The Skull laughed harshly.

WENTWORTH LAUGHED, too. The ropes were stubborn, but how could he wet them? How... He found out that the post was rough. It wouldn't saw through the ropes in anything less than an hour. But there were splinters that would cut flesh, and produce... *wetness.* Even if he got free of the ropes, what could he hope to accomplish—unarmed, and facing the Skull? Undoubtedly, there were many more men within call.

"Reproducing the sonics was simple for you, eh, Skull?" he said. "Simple for any man who is a wizard at electrical gadgets such as these fake skeletons you hang about...."

"Not all of them are fakes, my friend." The Skull spoke softly. "There is, for instance, the skeleton of Nona Malvern and of that other woman and child."

"Not all of the men are fakes," Wentworth acknowledged. "Some merely wear dark clothing with the bones painted on in phosphorescence. And you are not always merely a painted wooden box with a voice wired into it I think that now, for instance, you are merely wearing a dark robe and that you are present in fact."

"Is this evidence?" Impatience marked the Skull's voice. "Make an end… and sign the paper. I promise you a quick death. And the women. A head shot before you are stripped of flesh. Come, surely that is magnanimous of me?"

The splinters had not produced as much blood as Wentworth had hoped. He tore the flesh of his wrists. "To get the sonics that opened the gate," he hurried on, "you merely set up a recording device when you staged that riot near my house on the first night. You have been clever, and there is damnably little evidence against you. But once the finger of suspicion is pointed, the police can find evidence."

The Skull was moving toward him now, and his hands came out from the black robe he wore, producing a piece of paper. "You will sign this, Wentworth," he said shortly.

Wentworth said quietly, *"Go to hell, Mr. Samuel Wister!"*

The Skull stopped and the hands that were holding the paper trembled the least bit.

Wentworth was frantically struggling with the ropes. His hands were slippery now and the ropes were stretching just a little.

"Do you think, Wister," he said sharply, "that you can conceal all the evidences of the ambuscade among the trees on your place? The piercings in the tree trunks which, lighted up and seen through your gas cloud, looked like skeletons? The wire cable on which you floated your Skull must have been anchored somewhere. The police will find those things, Wister, when they open the papers I have mailed them. They will find that you had been using the money of your ward, Nona Malvern, and that will tell them why you killed her."

"You can't know that," the Skull whispered. "It isn't possible!"

Wentworth laughed sharply. His left hand was almost free. "No, I'll admit that was guess-work, Wister, but it had to be something like that. A clever dodge, too, to turn suspicion away from you. And that visit to me the next morning, revealing things you intended should be found out anyway; poisoning your own drugs because no one would suspect you of doing such a foolhardy thing. And you own the company which Forbes heads—*don't you, Wister?*"

WENTWORTH STRAINED violently and his left hand slipped out of the ropes. The Skull caught the movement and started to leap back... too late. Wentworth's left hand flew out and fastened into the throat beneath the plaster masque of the skull. His fingers bit in deeply, and he pulled the Skull toward him while he strained to wrench his right hand free.

He saw the Skull's hand jab under the robe and knew that it would come out with a gun... and he could not dodge. He was still roped fast to the post. He had only one hand, and he must not release that hold. His shoulders hunched as he threw strength into that arm, increasing the pressure.

The gun whipped out of Wister's pocket and Wentworth yanked the man toward him just as the revolver blasted. The bullet struck in his thigh. Frantically, Wentworth wrenched at Wister's throat. That wound would drain him of strength... and

161

Wister was bringing up the gun again. Frantically, Wentworth wrenched at his right hand, still bound to the post. There was a tearing pain that shot to his shoulder... but the hand came free!

Wincingly, Wentworth swung that injured right hand at Wister's body... and the gun spat flame again. The bullet caught Wentworth in the body this time. He felt numbness spreading over his chest, but the ropes were dropping down about his feet. He tried to take a step forward and stumbled. Wister wrenched free, ran toward the darkness. Wentworth struggled up and his leg gave way again. The gun spat... lancing flame toward the Spider but Wister's aim was not good this time. Not good enough....

Wentworth's breath was sobbing in his throat. He could not reach Wister, could not overtake him with his wounded leg. And, no matter how poor Wister's aim was, he could finish the execution easily enough from a safe distance. Desperately, Wentworth's eyes swung about the dark cellar. Probably, Wister was going for more men....

Wentworth's gaze fell on the stiff figure with the hose before the glass cages which held the girls prisoner. The figure had not moved. Eagerness sent Wentworth scrabbling toward it, as he guessed at the truth. Wister had not dared allow one of his men in the room while he forced the stock transfer from Wentworth. Probably, he had intended to lie and say he had not obtained it. At any rate, this figure poised before the cages was a skeleton—a human skeleton swung on delicate, almost invisible wires from the ceiling.

With a final scrambling leap, Wentworth reached the skeleton and seized from his hands the length of flexible metal hose. There was a valve. Even as Wentworth's hands closed upon the hose, the gun spoke again. Wentworth cried out and pitched limply down before the glass cages where Nita and Melissa were held inexorable prisoners.

Melissa had fainted. Nita was sobbing, crying out frantically as she struck her fragile hands against the glass that imprisoned her. If only she could break free! The Skull was coming forward at a run now. He held the gun in one hand, in the other the stock transfer.

"Don't worry," he rasped at Nita. "He isn't dead... yet. I'll wring enough life from him to sign this paper, and *afterward....*"

The gun was wary in his hand. He was watching for the slightest movement on the part of Wentworth. But when Wentworth moved, it was with explosive force, like the release of a tightly coiled spring. He sprang sideways like a crab and as he moved, the hose in his hand opened with a prolonged, strangled hiss!

There was an instant when the Skull's prolonged scream was all terror, and there was another when it changed to a shriek of titter clear agony. After that, there was no sound at all for a long, long space. It was in that sobbing silence that Wentworth heard distinctly the battering axes upon metal doors. His eyes swung to Nita. That could mean but one thing... the police."

"Dick," Nita sobbed. "Oh, Dick, you won, but... but you wore the clothes of the Spider. Your guns...."

"The guns are gone, stolen by the Skull," Wentworth panted. "Good lord, he... shot me with my own gun."

"But he captured the Spider, Dick," Nita cried. "The police must know that."

Wentworth was weak with the increasing pain of his wounds. "Yes," he said thickly, "the police know that. The police...."

WHEN THE final door crashed down, Donald Beck was the first man through. He crossed the room in a rush and stared at the grim signs of the fight. On the floor lay a man with a shattered false Skull over his head and his chest... his chest was stripped bare of flesh. Near him, Nita and Melissa were huddled over Wentworth who seemed unconscious with his wounds. And in one of those ominous glass cases was the skeleton of a man—a skeleton about whose feet lay the remnants of the Spider's black cape and hat.

A cop said, "Geez, look, he got the Spider. It's *got* to be the Spider! The crooks we caught say the Skull was in here all alone with the prisoners."

Donald Beck was on his knees beside Wentworth. "I hope you can forgive me, sir," he was pleading. "I—I made a mistake all along. I thought that you were the Spider. He was in league with the Skull. He kidnapped Melissa. Now, I can tell the truth about that racket money. Melissa, dear...."

Melissa smiled up faintly. "You were wonderful, darling," she said. "How did you ever find me?"

Beck flushed, "I saw the Spider and followed him. That's all."

Nita was bending over Wentworth and she bent low, whispering. "The wounds aren't bad, Dick. You can beat Toley's evidence easily now that we can prove Wister was the Skull, and... and his bullets are in your body. We just tell them that it must have been Wister's bullets he dug out of the trees."

Wentworth's smile was faint. He reached up his uninjured arm to pull Nita down to him. "Please, Nita," he said, and his smile grew whimsical. "It seems to me that I'm a hell of a crime buster, having to get shot with my own gun to clear myself. Can't you—won't you please tell me I'm wonderful, too?"

Nita laughed, softly, and her lips told Wentworth in a way that left no doubt at all what she thought.

THE SPIDER

❑ #1: The Spider Strikes	$13.95
❑ #2: The Wheel of Death	$13.95
❑ #3: Wings of the Black Death	$13.95
❑ #4: City of Flaming Shadows	$13.95
❑ #5: Empire of Doom!	$13.95
❑ #6: Citadel of Hell	$13.95
❑ #7: The Serpent of Destruction	$13.95
❑ #8: The Mad Horde	$13.95
❑ #9: Satan's Death Blast	$13.95
❑ #10: The Corpse Cargo	$13.95
❑ #11: Prince of the Red Looters	$13.95
❑ #12: Reign of the Silver Terror	$13.95
❑ #13: Builders of the Dark Empire	$13.95
❑ #14: Death's Crimson Juggernaut	$13.95
❑ #15: The Red Death Rain	$13.95
❑ #16: The City Destroyer	$13.95
❑ #17: The Pain Emperor	$13.95
❑ #18: The Flame Master	$13.95
❑ #19: Slaves of the Crime Master	$13.95
❑ #20: Reign of the Death Fiddler	$13.95
❑ #21: Hordes of the Red Butcher	$13.95
❑ #22: Dragon Lord of the Underworld	$13.95
❑ #23: Master of the Death-Madness	$13.95
❑ #24: King of the Red Killers	$13.95
❑ #25: Overlord of the Damned	$13.95
❑ #26: Death Reign of the Vampire King	$13.95
❑ #27: Emperor of the Yellow Death	$13.95
❑ #28: The Mayor of Hell	$13.95
❑ #29: Slaves of the Murder Syndicate	$13.95
❑ #30: Green Globes of Death	$13.95
❑ #31: The Cholera King	$13.95
❑ #32: Slaves of the Dragon	$13.95
❑ #33: Legions of Madness	$12.95
❑ #34: Laboratory of the Damned	$12.95
❑ #35: Satan's Sightless Legion	$12.95
❑ #36: The Coming of the Terror	$12.95
❑ #37: The Devil's Death-Dwarfs	$12.95
❑ #38: City of Dreadful Night	$12.95
❑ #39: Reign of the Snake Men	$12.95
❑ #40: Dictator of the Damned	$12.95
❑ #41: The Mill-Town Massacres	$12.95
❑ #42: Satan's Workshop	$12.95
❑ #43: Scourge of the Yellow Fangs	$12.95
❑ #44: The Devil's Pawnbroker	$12.95
❑ #45: Voyage of the Coffin Ship	$12.95

❑ #46: The Man Who Ruled in Hell	$13.95
❑ #47: Slaves of the Black Monarch	$13.95
❑ #48: Machineguns Over the White House	$13.95
❑ #49: The City That Dared Not Eat	$13.95
❑ #50: Master of the Flaming Horde	$13.95
❑ #51: Satan's Switchboard	$13.95
❑ #52: Legions of the Accursed Light	$13.95
❑ #53: The City of Lost Men	$13.95
❑ #54: The Grey Horde Creeps	$13.95
❑ #55: City of Whispering Death	$13.95
❑ #56: When Thousands Slept in Hell	$13.95
❑ #57: Satan's Shakles	$14.95
❑ #58: The Emperor From Hell	$14.95
❑ #59: The Devil's Candlesticks	$14.95
❑ #60: The City That Paid to Die	$14.95
❑ #61: The Spider at Bay	$14.95
❑ #62: Scourge of the Black Legions	$14.95
❑ #63: The Withering Death	$14.95
❑ #64: Claws of the Golden Dragon	$14.95
❑ #65: The Song of Death	$14.95
❑ #66: The Silver Death Reign	$14.95
❑ #67: Blight of the Blazing Eye	$14.95
❑ *NEW:* #68: King of the Fleshless Legion	$14.95

THE WESTERN RAIDER

❑ #1: Guns of the Damned	$13.95
❑ #2: The Hawk Rides Back from Death	$13.95
❑ #3: Gun-Call for the Lost Legion	$13.95
❑ #4: The Law of Silver Trent	$13.95
❑ #5: The Gun-Prayer of Silver Trent	$13.95
❑ #6: Silver Trent Rides Alone	$13.95

G-8 AND HIS BATTLE ACES

❑ #1: The Bat Staffel	$13.95

CAPTAIN SATAN

❑ #1: The Mask of the Damned	$13.95
❑ #2: Parole for the Dead	$13.95
❑ #3: The Dead Man Express	$13.95
❑ #4: A Ghost Rides the Dawn	$13.95
❑ #5: The Ambassador From Hell	$13.95

DR. YEN SIN

❑ #1: Mystery of the Dragon's Shadow	$12.95
❑ #2: Mystery of the Golden Skull	$12.95
❑ #3: Mystery of the Singing Mummies	$12.95

POPULAR HERO PULPS AVAILABLE NOW:

ACE G-MAN
- ❏ #1: The Suicide Squad Reports for Death $14.95
- ❏ #2: Coffins for the Suicide Squad $14.95
- ❏ #3: Shells for the Suicide Squad $14.95
- ❏ #4: The Suicide Squad in Corpse-Town $14.95
- ❏ #5: Wanted–In Three Pine Coffins $14.95
- ❏ *NEW:* #6: The Suicide Squad's Dawn Patrol $14.95

OPERATOR 5
- ❏ #1: The Masked Invasion $13.95
- ❏ #2: The Invisible Empire $13.95
- ❏ #3: The Yellow Scourge $13.95
- ❏ #4: The Melting Death $13.95
- ❏ #5: Cavern of the Damned $13.95
- ❏ #6: Master of Broken Men $13.95
- ❏ #7: Invasion of the Dark Legions $13.95
- ❏ #8: The Green Death Mists $13.95
- ❏ #9: Legions of Starvation $13.95
- ❏ #10: The Red Invader $13.95
- ❏ #11: The League of War-Monsters $13.95
- ❏ #12: The Army of the Dead $13.95
- ❏ #13: March of the Flame Marauders $13.95
- ❏ #14: Blood Reign of the Dictator $13.95
- ❏ #15: Invasion of the Yellow Warlords $13.95
- ❏ #16: Legions of the Death Master $13.95
- ❏ #17: Hosts of the Flaming Death $13.95
- ❏ #18: Invasion of the Crimson Death Cult $13.95
- ❏ #19: Attack of the Blizzard Men $13.95
- ❏ #20: Scourge of the Invisible Death $13.95
- ❏ #21: Raiders of the Red Death $13.95
- ❏ #22: War-Dogs of the Green Destroyer $13.95
- ❏ #23: Rockets From Hell $13.95
- ❏ #24: War-Masters from the Orient $13.95
- ❏ #25: Crime's Reign of Terror $13.95
- ❏ #26: Death's Ragged Army $13.95
- ❏ #27: Patriots' Death Battalion $13.95
- ❏ #28: The Bloody Forty-five Days $13.95
- ❏ #29: America's Plague Battalions $13.95
- ❏ #30: Liberty's Suicide Legions $13.95
- ❏ #31: Siege of the Thousand Patriots $13.95
- ❏ #32: Patriots' Death March $14.95
- ❏ #33: Revolt of the Lost Legions $14.95
- ❏ #34: Drums of Destruction $14.95
- ❏ #35: The Army Without a Country $14.95
- ❏ #36: The Bloody Frontiers $14.95
- ❏ #37: The Coming of the Mongol Hordes $14.95

CAPTAIN COMBAT
- ❏ #1: The Sky Beast of Berlin $13.95
- ❏ #2: Red Wings For the Blood Battalion $13.95
- ❏ #3: Low Ceiling For Nazi Hell Hawks $13.95

DUSTY AYRES AND HIS BATTLE BIRDS
- ❏ #1: Black Lightning! $13.95
- ❏ #2: Crimson Doom $13.95
- ❏ #3: The Purple Tornado $13.95
- ❏ #4: The Screaming Eye $13.95
- ❏ #5: The Green Thunderbolt $13.95
- ❏ #6: The Red Destroyer $13.95
- ❏ #7: The White Death $13.95
- ❏ #8: The Black Avenger $13.95
- ❏ #9: The Silver Typhoon $13.95
- ❏ #10: The Troposphere F-S $13.95
- ❏ #11: The Blue Cyclone $13.95
- ❏ #12: The Tesla Raiders $13.95

MAVERICKS
- ❏ #1: Five Against the Law $12.95
- ❏ #2: Mesquite Manhunters $12.95
- ❏ #3: Bait for the Lobo Pack $12.95
- ❏ #4: Doc Grimson's Outlaw Posse $12.95
- ❏ #5: Charlie Parr's Gunsmoke Cure $12.95

THE MYSTERIOUS WU FANG
- ❏ #1: The Case of the Six Coffins $12.95
- ❏ #2: The Case of the Scarlet Feather $12.95
- ❏ #3: The Case of the Yellow Mask $12.95
- ❏ #4: The Case of the Suicide Tomb $12.95
- ❏ #5: The Case of the Green Death $12.95
- ❏ #6: The Case of the Black Lotus $12.95
- ❏ #7: The Case of the Hidden Scourge $12.95

THE SECRET 6
- ❏ #1: The Red Shadow $13.95
- ❏ #2: House of Walking Corpses $13.95
- ❏ #3: The Monster Murders $13.95
- ❏ #4: The Golden Alligator $13.95

CAPTAIN ZERO
- ❏ #1: City of Deadly Sleep $13.95
- ❏ #2: The Mark of Zero! $13.95
- ❏ #3: The Golden Murder Syndicate $13.95